No Promises in the Wind

This is the United States in 1932. It is a world in which fifteen-year-old Josh Grondowski must make his way. Haggard and beaten men wait beside a factory gate for work that isn't there. Anxious-eyed women wait on breadlines, desperately trying to feed their families.

Grinding poverty creates fear and anger, and hopeless rage, where there should be love. It destroyed many homes.

This is the powerful and disturbing story of one such family. What happens when two boys are forced to strike out on their own: What kindness and savagery they met on the road, and how their determined struggle to survive taught them tolerance and tenderness.

Tempo Books by Irene Hunt

ACROSS FIVE APRILS
THE LOTTERY ROSE
NO PROMISES IN THE WIND
UP A ROAD SLOWLY
WILLIAM

NO IRENE HUNT
PROMISES
IN THE WIND

TEMPO BOOKS, NEW YORK

This Tempo Book contains the complete
text of the original hardcover edition.

NO PROMISES IN THE WIND

A Tempo Book / published by arrangement with
Follett Publishing Company

PRINTING HISTORY
Follett Publishing Company edition published in 1970
Sixteenth Tempo printing / August 1985

ISBN: 0-441-58869-7

Tempo Books are published by The Berkley Publishing Group,
200 Madison Avenue, New York, New York 10016.
Tempo Books are registered in the United States Patent Office.
PRINTED IN THE UNITED STATES OF AMERICA

Chapter One

Joey stirred on his side of our bed when the alarm clock jangled at a quarter to four. "You want me to go with you, Josh?" he asked sleepily.

I reached out to the bedside table, stopped the alarm, snapped on the shaded study lamp, and lay back on my pillow. The chill of early October had sharpened during the night, and the discomfort of being cold together with too few hours of sleep made me irritable and moody. I didn't even feel particularly grateful to Joey for offering to go with me. In the first place he wasn't a lot of help, and anyway, three hours of delivering papers in the dark city streets was too hard for him though he'd never have admitted it. Joey had been frail since he was a baby, but he was tough. He'd have

7

been up in a minute if I had said, yes, I needed his help.

As it was, I didn't answer his question and he sighed deeply as he turned his face away from the light. I couldn't tell whether that sigh was one of relief at being able to go back to sleep or one of hurt at my rudeness. Ashamed, I got up and found an extra blanket which I threw over him and tucked around his shoulders. I could sense his feeling of comfort as he curled up into a tight little spiral and snuggled down under the extra warmth.

When I was dressed, I sat down in the big mohair chair beside the window, twisting my body to avoid the broken spring in the chair's back. "Just five minutes," I told myself, "just five minutes to rest and get used to being awake."

I stared at the faded paper on the wall in front of me without really seeing it until I became conscious of the yellowed figures of cowboys riding their broncs in precise paths from baseboard to ceiling. My mother had allowed me to select that paper five years before when I was no older than Joey, and I had held out for cowboys and broncs, scorning Mom's preference for pots of flowers or bright colored birds. I studied the horses and their daredevil riders for a long time as if they mattered. They didn't, of course, but concentrating on them kept me awake.

Finally I roused myself. My paper route didn't mean much money, but it was important. Dad had been out of work for eight months, and only the day before, my sister had received notice of a cut-back in personnel which cost her the clerking job she'd had for nearly a year. Every few pennies counted in our family; a job was a job, and to risk losing it by being late was out of the question.

It was dark in the kitchen when I went downstairs, but I could see the outline of my mother's figure as she stood at the stove. "Why did you get up, Mom?" I asked gruffly. "I tell you over and over—"

She put her hand on my arm. "Hush, Josh, let's not wake Dad. He couldn't sleep until about two hours ago." She poured out a cup of hot milk and handed it to me. "Here, drink this; I'll have a little breakfast for you at seven."

She was not as tall as I was; she had to lift her face when she kissed my cheek. "I'm so proud that Miss Crowne wants you to play for the school assembly next week. I'm very proud of you, Josh."

"I wish you could come and hear us. Howie and I are going pretty good lately."

"I know. I want to hear you so much—but, then, I can't and there's no use talking about it." She turned back to the stove and moved some pans aimlessly. "You can stay after school and practice if you want to. There isn't much for you to do around here."

My mother ironed all day in the laundry a few

blocks down the street. She shouldn't have been doing work like that. She played piano beautifully, and for a long time she had given lessons to children in our neighborhood until recently when no one had money to pay for a luxury like music. She taught me for seven years, up until I was thirteen and we had to sell the piano at the time Dad's work at the factory was cut to three days a week. She understood my love for music and she encouraged it—always there was encouragement from my mother.

Dad had mixed feelings about my playing. He loved music too, really; it was a common love of music that had drawn him and Mom together when she was a black-haired little Irish girl of eighteen and he was a Polish widower almost twice her age. Dad's parents had been musicians in Poland, good ones too, but poor as far as money was concerned. There had been poverty in Dad's childhood, and he placed the blame for it upon a father who had never been able to leave his music for the toil of farm or mine or factory. I had heard him talking to Mom about his feelings toward men making music a means of livelihood.

"These hands, Mary," he had said, spreading his own hands in front of her, "these are a man's hands. They've become calloused and they've been split sometimes, and bleeding. But they've never dawdled over a keyboard while you and the children suffered."

Mom came quickly to my defense. "Josh is a

worker too, Stefan. A boy who has gone out to deliver papers on bitter winter mornings since he was ten is no soft child. Your son is much like you. He respects hard work, but there's no reason why work must deny him the gift he has inherited from both of us. He's quick, Stefan, and he learns so naturally. We mustn't deny him."

He usually agreed with her in earlier years, sometimes grudgingly, but without rancor. As times grew harder, though, and work became a matter of the highest importance in the minds of most people, Dad's impatience with my practicing became bitter. Sometimes it seemed to me that his impatience with my every act or word became bitter.

The year 1932 was not a good one in which to be fifteen years old and in close quarters with a hopeless father. I was not young and appealing to people as Joey was; I was not docile and quiet like Kitty. Dad and I clashed during the year, often and with greater anger as the hard times continued.

It hadn't always been that way. In the early years of my life I had been the young prince in our home. I was Dad's first son, and he was a man for whom sons were a symbol of his own strength and manhood. He was a very kind father to Kitty, who was the child of his first marriage, but he couldn't help being a little cocky about his son. He used to take me everywhere—out to the ball parks, to the amusement park where I could try every ride and eat popcorn to my fill, down to the

11

plant to meet his friends who thought my old-fashioned name and sober face were funny. I used to hear Dad bragging to them, "You should see this boy eat. It's all Mary and I can do to keep him full of milk and potatoes. What we'll do when he's fifteen, I don't know."

And that was true—he didn't know. By the time I was fifteen, the problem of a healthy appetite was no longer funny.

We went through some bad times beginning with the year I was five, the year Joey was born. My brother was a sickly baby, given only a slim chance of living. Mom and Dad wore themselves out that year, taking turns at sitting up all night to rescue Joey from strangling spasms that threatened to snuff his life out. There were huge doctor bills and anxiety over money as well as the puny child; there was great fatigue for both my parents, and Dad was not a man who took hardship or physical discomfort quietly. If I forgot that Joey was asleep and came into the house banging doors and yelling as I'd always done, Dad would turn on me in a way that soon convinced me he'd lost all the love for me he'd ever had. Kitty escaped much of his frustration, being older and gentler by nature. She used to play quiet games with me and take me for long walks to keep me away from the baby's room. I loved Kitty very much, Kitty and Mom, but a harshness sprang up between Dad and me during the first years of Joey's life. Somehow that harshness increased with time, intensified by the unyielding coldness I felt toward Dad, a stubborn unwillingness ever to respond to his attempts toward regaining my affection.

Those attempts grew more infrequent as times grew worse. In 1930 there were fewer and fewer hours of work each week for Dad; in 1932 he lost his job completely. With that loss, with the loss of his savings when the bank closed, maybe with the loss of being the proud man he'd once been, Dad's attitude toward me grew less and less like that of a father who loves his son.

He was a man who had liked to talk about how he had pulled himself up by his own bootstraps, how he, a poor immigrant in 1910, had risen to be foreman at work, had a small, neat home with a mortgage gradually dwindling, was able to take his family for Sunday rides in his own automobile, could buy his wife an electric sewing machine for Christmas. And if he could do all this, was there any reason why others couldn't? None whatever, except that those who hadn't done as well were lazy, improvident, or stupid.

And then suddenly, his bootstraps, his industry, his shrewdness and thriftiness, were worth nothing. He was as powerless to save his home, to feed his family properly, to feel an ounce of pride or confidence in himself as any man he had scorned in former years.

It was hard for Dad, I knew, but his unreasonable rages in which I was usually the whipping boy bewildered me at first and then angered me deeply. Mom had talked with me many times about him.

"We must be patient with him, Josh. He's a good man—just wrong in letting his desperation get the better of his reason. We mustn't forget the goodness in him just because we can't go along with some of the things—we are sorry about." She never would actually come out and agree with me that Dad had done anything wrong. It was always, "I know, Josh. I know, dear. Let's just be a little patient."

That morning as we stood in the dark kitchen together I made a vow that I'd try to be patient with Dad if only for her sake. She was so little, so bent with weariness and worry that I felt a great tenderness for her. I patted her shoulder as I placed my empty cup on the table. "Get another hour of rest, Mom. You don't have to be up before six." She nodded, but I knew she wouldn't go back to bed. She'd be afraid of oversleeping, of failing to have breakfast ready as each of her family made an appearance in the kitchen. She worked too hard, cared too much about the rest of us. It worried me. And to give Dad credit, I must admit it worried him too.

They were sitting together, Mom and Dad, at the kitchen table when I got back. He looked beaten and disheveled, but not angry as he so often did. He was holding Mom's hand, and they were talking quietly when I came into the room.

14

Mom got up to fix the breakfast she had promised three hours before. "We have a few eggs this morning," she said. Then she noticed that I shivered as I drew close to the stove. "Oh, Josh, you didn't wear your sweater. Didn't you see that I had it laid out on the chair for you? These mornings are too chilly for—"

Her words touched off Dad's ready anger. He turned toward me furiously. "Must your mother dress you like you are three years old again? Must she be worried with all her other worries because you show no responsiblity—even for wearing the right clothes? It will be fine, won't it, when you catch a cold and we have doctor's bills on top of everything else?"

I started to say something that blazed up inside me, something about the fact that I was at least earning a little to buy food for us, but I caught the pleading in Mom's face and I kept quiet. Dad sat for a moment, looking from one of us to the other. Then he got up and put his arms around Mom.

"Forgive, Mary. Please forgive. Why do I say things to the boy that hurt you? I think there is a meanness in me—"

"No, Stefan, there's a tiredness in you—and hunger. Won't you eat one of the eggs, please? I'll scramble the other two for the children to divide amongst themselves."

"No, I don't want anything more. I'll go now and meet the other men. We're going to try a

15

place out on Western Avenue." He looked at me. I had a feeling that he wanted to say "Forgive" to me as he had to Mom, but for the life of me I couldn't have accepted an apology at that moment. I turned away from him abruptly. He had lashed out at me too many times, too unreasonably. I didn't feel the love for him that Mom did.

When he was gone, I turned to her. "Don't fix any breakfast for me, Mom. It would choke me."

She didn't answer. She just walked to the window and stared outside. I went up to my room, finished some homework, and got ready for school.

When I came down, she had a sandwich of bread and oleomargarine for me. "Buy a cup of hot cocoa and have this for lunch, Josh. You can't play very well for Miss Crowne if you're starved."

She turned away quickly after she had spoken and hurried out of the kitchen as if she feared I might mention what had happened earlier. I stood at the kitchen table, looking at the sandwich she had made for me. I wanted to ask her if *she* had money for a cup of hot cocoa after a morning of ironing. But I heard the door of her room close sharply, and I knew the meaning of that sound. I'd heard it often at times when I was younger and she was fed up with my childish demands for attention. It meant, "Keep your distance. I am not available for further conversation."

I didn't think she was angry with me this time, but I had an idea she didn't want to hear me say anything against Dad. Slowly I put the sandwich into the pocket of my jacket and started out for school.

Penn High School had become a refuge for me. I was a good student, and that helped to make school attractive. I wasn't one of the popular set, but that didn't bother me because when classes were over, the piano up in Miss Crowne's music room was mine, and Howie was with me.

I played better than most kids of my age, I guess. That was partly because I loved music better than anything on earth. I played by the hour, improvising upon the snatches of melody that ran through my mind, fumbling sometimes, faking at others, but finally finding something that sounded beautiful and right to me. When that happened, I rearranged and polished and worked at it until the notes went slipping under my fingers like water.

Howie shared my love of music, and he was one of those rare musicians. He seemed to have been born with an instinct for understanding music, for hearing it precisely and then reproducing it with a little something extra, all his own. Without being able to read a note, he could coax music out of a piano, a guitar, a mouth organ, a pocket comb. His favorite instrument, though, was the banjo. He had an old one which he once told me he had stolen, and that was very likely true. However he came by it, that banjo meant more to Howie than anything on earth. He knew how to make those

17

strings sing, and we hadn't practiced together very long until we were making music that sent splinters of delight all through me. With music like that I could forget the anxieties at home; I could forget Dad's moods and the cheerless faces everywhere on Chicago's grim west side. Day after day Howie and I closed the door of the music room and shut out the troubled times.

Howie was a boy of many sorrows, but he was one that sorrow couldn't quite pin down. He was only a few months younger than I was, but not much taller than Joey. He was a thin-faced, sallow boy with great dark eyes that could look mournful one minute and full of laughter the next as if they mocked mournfulness and refused to accept it. I guess he had never known his father; he'd had a line of stepfathers, none of whom cared much about him. His mother was drunk when she could find money to buy whiskey; when she wasn't drunk, she was mean. Howie didn't talk about her much. He liked to talk of things that made for laughter, and the most striking feature about him was his mouth, a mouth that seemed always eager to laugh. Maybe I noticed that especially because my own mouth was characteristically unsmiling, even a little sullen. He was a wonderful guy, that Howie, the only real friend I had in high school.

That afternoon we were practicing something I had composed. It was a fluid, changing tone-story, a theme that I improvised upon according to my

mood, an outpouring of feelings that were inside
me and changed with the quality of sunlight or
the lack of it, with the dreams that sometimes
seemed to be possible, with the despair that was a
part of the times. It was something Howie and I
had worked on for months, and lately when we'd
played it, Miss Crowne's face glowed. We didn't
have to ask her if we were good. We knew we
were when she asked us to play for the school
assembly.

The October afternoon outside the windows
was as gentle and drowsy as if there weren't a
trouble in the world. For all old Nature knew or
cared, every able-bodied man the length and
width of the country had a good-paying job; every
supper table in the country had enough on it to
satisfy the hunger of the children gathered
around it. Nature might even have carelessly supposed that the hunger of the children was an
indifferent kind of hunger, sharp enough from
work or play, but nothing to be scared about. The
jab of hunger pangs was nothing to panic over
when the smell of a good supper at twilight was
as much expected and as little considered as twilight itself, or the light of morning. That is the
way it had been with me once—wonderful,
ravenous, *indifferent* hunger. It was no longer like
that for a great many of us.

I was suddenly angered that Nature could be so
carefree, so oblivious to the dreariness that my
music only brightened for minutes. I struck a few

chords on the yellow keys, full of a helpless kind
of resentment, but Howie brought me out of my
mood in seconds.

"What's itchin' at you, Joshaway?" he asked,
laughing at me. "Come on, let's get goin'. This
banjo's got a deep, low yearnin' for something
with a Dixieland beat." His fingers skittered over
the strings as he spoke.

I grinned at him and brought my hands down
on the keyboard, ready for the opening bars of
our number. All the months of playing together
had made Howie and me like one boy when we
swung into our music. He could sense the moment
when I'd go into a change of tempo; he knew
when my mood called for laughter and clowning,
or when it began to sink low, low down into the
blues of men who cowered around the wire trash
baskets on street corners and warmed themselves
with burning newspapers. Howie and I vibrated
with music that neither of us could have talked
about in musical terms.

Miss Crowne must have been bone-tired that
afternoon. Her face looked faintly gray and
drawn, but she came into the room and stood
there watching us, swaying a little with our
rhythm, smiling and brushing tears out of her
eyes at the same time. When we were through,
she walked over and stood beside the piano.

Howie was a ham—there was no doubt about
that. He laid his head against the back of his
chair and closed his eyes. "Lord, wasn't that
20

sweet! Josh, you're terrific, and I'm mighty near as good as you."

Miss Crowne laughed then; she often laughed at Howie. "You two all but make me forget the bread lines for a few minutes." She nodded at me. "It's good, Josh, real good. You're making it come alive, and Howie is giving it a beat that's going to make the assembly sit up and listen next week."

When Miss Crowne praised us, we felt clouds under our feet. Although she made a gesture of brushing us outside the door when we lingered over our thanks for the use of her room, we were confident that she liked us, that she was proud of what we were doing.

"Get on home now, you two," she told us. "You have homework, and I have an hour's ride on the streetcar. Get going, gentlemen."

We had to go, although we hated leaving her. We wanted to stay and hear again how much she liked our music. Mostly, I guess, we wanted to put off the hour when we had to go back to our families.

Outside I said good-bye to Howie and told him that maybe I could get out that evening in which case I'd meet him at the usual place by the corner drugstore. I didn't say that I'd get out if Dad was in a mood to ignore me. I didn't have to explain; Howie knew how things were.

He said, "Bring Joey along. I snitched a jigsaw puzzle the other day from someone who'll never miss it. I want to give it to Joey."

21

I shrugged. "He has to go to bed early," I said. I didn't care to have a younger brother tagging after me. Howie didn't mind. He had no brothers of his own, and he had a special kind of affection for Joey.

Joey was, of course, the protected and best-loved one of us at home. He had grown stronger with the years, but he was still fragile, a little too slender and delicate for the lean times. He was also beautiful, a golden child with a mouth that looked as if it had been sculptured, and great gray eyes under his shock of bright hair. I loved Joey's beauty, but I wasn't cured of the old resentment toward Joey himself. His birth had meant the end of happiness between Dad and me. I suppose I should have been a little wiser, but as the years went by, it didn't occur to me to bring reason to my feelings. I just went on thoughtlessly, not exactly disliking my brother, but not liking him much either.

I took Joey's hero-worship for me with indifference just as for years I had taken such things as food and shelter and security for granted. It was obvious that Joey thought of me as a great guy. I was strong and husky; I knew things that made him feel I was pretty brilliant. I could do things he thought it would be great to do, and he didn't seem to mind that I was often brusque with him, that I lorded it over him with an authority I had no right to claim. Maybe Joey accepted these things as the way of all big brothers. I don't

know. But I do know that a thrust of guilt sometimes hit me where I lived when I looked at his
face and saw the eager friendliness there which I
knew I didn't always deserve.

It was like that when I came upon him after my
practice session at school. He was sitting in the
alley back of our house, bending over something
in the darkness. I couldn't see what he was up to
until I was almost on top of him. There he sat in
the midst of dirt and trash, and directly in front
of him was a lean alley cat which he stroked as it
lapped milk from a rusty pan. A five-cent milk
bottle was in Joey's hand.

"She was just about starved, Josh," he said
quickly as if realizing that he must come up with
an explanation. Joey knew well enough that milk
was not for alley cats that fall. "She's got babies,
and she needs milk awful bad. You're not mad at
me, are you?"

"Where did you get a nickel for milk?" I asked
sternly.

"Kitty gave it to me. She walked home from
the elevated yesterday to save streetcar fare, and
she gave me the nickel because she couldn't buy
me a present for my birthday last week. It was
my nickel, Josh, honest. And the mother cat was
so hungry."

"Kitty's in big business giving you a nickel
when she's just been laid off her job," I answered.
"And you listen to me, Joey—when you get hold
of a nickel, you give it to Mom to help with

23

groceries. I don't know what Dad would do to you if he knew you'd bought milk for a mangy alley cat."

Joey looked scared. Petted as he'd always been, he still hadn't wholly escaped Dad's mean moods that year. "Are you going to tell on me, Josh?" he asked.

I shook my head. "There's enough trouble in our house without adding to it. Just don't do it again. Just don't *ever* do a thing like this again."

Even in what I felt was justifiable anger, my words struck something inside me. "A thing like this" meant feeding a starving animal, and I was making Joey feel that he had committed a crime in being compassionate. Once I had been as eager as he was to feed every stray animal that came near us. It was strange what poverty and fear of hunger could do to a sense of decency.

I guess my voice softened a little. "Come on, Joey, let's go inside. I won't say anything about this."

We went inside to desolation. Mom was lifting boiled potatoes from the pan to a serving dish which she placed upon the table. Nothing else was there except glasses of milk at Kitty's place and at Joey's and mine. There was a cup of coffee at Dad's place, nothing at Mom's. Dad stood in front of the chair where Kitty was sitting, his face dark and forbidding. Kitty was crying.

"I tried, Daddy," she was saying. "I tried so hard. I wanted that job more than I've ever wanted anything in my life. I was so scared that I just went to pieces. I couldn't remember my short-hand, and my hands shook so that I couldn't do the typing test. You've got to believe me, Daddy, I tried—"

"Well, you didn't try hard enough, my girl, and get that into your head right now. Your mother and I have spent good money putting you through high school, giving you a chance to learn this stuff so you could make a living. You'll go down to the Loop tomorrow and you'll try about a hundred times harder than you tried today or you need-n't—"

He stopped himself suddenly and sat down at the table, looking as desperate as I'd ever seen him. Kitty sobbed. It was awful.

I had never known Dad to be mean to Kitty. She was the child of his Elzbieta, the young wife who had died in Poland when Kitty was born. Mom had told me many times about the fright-ened little girl Kitty had been when Dad sent for her to come to this country and to a new mother. I guess Dad and Mom had worked hard in those days to bolster Kitty's confidence with love and understanding.

"You must understand, Josh," Mom had told me once when I thought Kitty had been treated with more consideration than I had. "You must understand that Dad is terribly proud of you. You're a son, and Dad is a man who wants sons. But sometimes he's afraid of showing all he feels

25

for you—he'll lean over backward to show his girl-child that he's just as proud of her. He'll even go so far that it seems he's setting her up above you, but it's not so. You'll have to understand this thing in Dad's nature."

That night as Kitty cried I wondered if Dad was capable of loving anyone.

It was only a few minutes until he turned on me. "And where have *you* been until nearly dark?" he demanded. "Why is it you don't get home after school to help your mother?"

"I was practicing," I answered shortly, expecting this admission to bring more wrath down on me, but Mom quickly interrupted. "I gave him permission to stay after school, Stefan; he needed to practice for the assembly program next week."

He didn't say anything after that; he just sat huddled in his chair, staring at the plate in front of him.

We were all silent for a long time. Joey kept his eyes lowered and ate very slowly. I felt pretty sure that he understood why I had chosen to say nothing to Dad about the nickel's worth of milk that had gone to a hungry cat.

Then I did something which called forth more wrath than Joey's gift to the cat would have done. It was thoughtless, of course, but I was always hungry, and many times at the supper table I had asked the same question: "Are there any more potatoes, Mom?"

Dad turned on me as if I had struck him. "No,

there aren't any more potatoes, and if you haven't had enough, that is just too damned bad. Do you think your paltry little job gives you special privileges to eat when everyone else at the table is hungry, too? Do you realize that your mother ironed all day to buy the food set before us, that *she* never asks for second helpings?"

Mom tried to stop him. She said, "Stefan, Stefan, has it come to this? Are we watching what one another swallows?"

He got up then and stalked outside. Kitty ran up to her room, and Joey went outside to sit on the steps. Mom and I sat alone at the table. She didn't cry—I guess she was long past crying. She just sat there without speaking, and I sat looking at her and wondering.

She had always been so pretty, so young, until the past two years. Now she looked old, although actually she was only thirty-six. I wondered how she could stand up in the face of all these troubles. I had my life at school, my music. Mom no longer had the music she loved—just an ironing board all day and a husband who made life miserable for his family when he came home at night.

"A great guy, Mom, a real great guy. Someone I must always look up to—is that what you're going to tell me?"

"Do you know what he's been through today, Josh? He's stood in line from seven-thirty this morning until five tonight to get into a factory

27

over on Western Avenue. He didn't have a bite to eat at noon, and only coffee and bread this morning—"

"That's all you've had too, isn't it?"

She ignored that. "He was fourth in line when they closed the window at the employment office. Can't you understand what that does to a man, Josh? Dad has always been able to feed us well, to clothe us and give us a good home. Now he's at bay. He's cornered and desperate."

"All of which gives him a right to hate Kitty and me."

"Josh, he doesn't hate either of you. He's always been tender with Kitty, and underneath his rough ways, he's so proud of you. If only you could understand how proud he's been . . ."

I was almost as angry with her as I was with him. "Do you know any more nice little stories, Mom? Do you know any more pretty speeches to make me love my dear old dad?" I got up and walked around the table to stand directly in front of her. "Listen to me, Mom. You heard the way he talked to us. You know that I can't make a move without having him bellow at me. And yet, in your book, he's still someone I must be patient with, someone I must love and honor—is that right?"

She looked at me steadily as I glared down at her. "When a woman sides with her children against her husband, a marriage and a family are all in ruins, Josh. Your father is crazed with fear and terror. I'll stand by him no matter what his son says about him."

"Then I don't think there's any place here for me. I'd better get out on my own. Isn't that right, Mom?"

I had never seen such suffering in her face as I saw then, but there was a hardness inside me that made me callous to that suffering. I repeated my question: "It's time I got out, isn't it, Mom?"

She nodded; at least it seemed she did. It was an almost imperceptible movement. "You're forcing me, Josh; you're driving me to say a thing that kills me. But I guess you're right. There's nothing here for you, no food, no jobs. And you and your father—it's better that you be apart before there's a sharper tragedy than we've yet known. I guess you're right. You're a strong boy; you're bright. Maybe you can find something better than what we have here."

She had said it. If I wanted to wallow in self-pity, I could say that both my father and mother had rejected me, had turned me out on my own. The world of that depression year lay ahead of me. If I licked it, fine; if I didn't, there wouldn't be anyone who cared.

But I wasn't nearly so desolate as I tried to convince myself that I should be. Actually I was suddenly filled with excitement, with an eagerness to get away, to break all the ties of home and to leave Chicago behind me forever. Plans began growing in my mind as I ran down the front steps

29

past Joey and into the street. I could hardly wait. I was breathless when I reached the drugstore and sat down on the curb in front to wait for Howie.

Chapter Two

Howie was a little late in joining me. He'd spent a half hour rummaging through a pile of crates which some grocery company had dumped on a vacant lot; it had been a half hour well spent, though, for he'd beaten the rats to an orange, only half decayed. He cut out the bad part with his pocketknife and divided what was left between us, smiling his big smile, full of pleasure that he was able to give me a treat. I wondered if Joey's cat had been as grateful for her pan of milk as I was for that bite of orange.

After a minute I told Howie of my plans. "I can't take it any longer," I told him. "I'm hittin' the roads, and I hope I never see Chicago again. Or my dad. Or"—bitterness rolled up like a fist and pounded inside me—"or my mother either," I added. "She's all for the old man. Well, I'll clear out. They can't be any happier to get rid of me than I am to be through with them."

Howie shrugged. I suppose my family difficulties seemed rather bland to him. Then he answered as casually as if I'd suggested walking around the block. "Well, I guess I'll be goin' with you, Josh."

"But what about your mother?"

Howie's eyes could get icy. "Are you tryin' to be funny?" he asked.

"No. I just want to be sure that someone isn't going to set the cops on the trail of two runaways."

"Well, be at ease."

We were silent for a minute. Then I said, "We can make it, can't we, Howie?"

He came out of his icy mood into a gay enthusiasm as if he'd done a mental handspring. "Of course we can make it. You know, in a way we're a couple of the luckiest guys around here because we've got something that people want. No matter how hard times are, people still want music. And we've got it, Josh. We're a notch or two above just 'pretty good,' and you know it. We'll find some place—a speakeasy, a restaurant, a dance hall—some place where people will pay to hear the kind of music we make."

I felt excitement growing in me. "We'll head for the smaller towns, Howie. Chicago's too big and ugly—Chicago's too close to my old man.

We'll head for the smaller towns that maybe aren't hit so hard."

"Right. The smaller towns. West. Maybe south and west where the winters won't be so long. Lord, I've been wantin' to see the West all my days. We'll pick us out an empty boxcar—"

We were feverish with our plans. We talked excitedly, interrupting one another with new ideas. Nothing seemed impossible during that hour when Howie and I sat on the curb and made our plans.

Then there was suddenly a distraction. I had paid no attention to the shadowy figure of a boy approaching until he stopped and stood before us. It was my brother.

"What are you doing here, Joey?" I asked gruffly.

"I'm going with you, Josh," he said as quietly as Howie had spoken an hour before.

"How do you know I'm going anywhere?"

"I know you're going to leave home—I heard you tell Mom. And you listen to me, Josh. I'm going with you."

"And you listen to me, Joey. You're going to do nothing of the sort. You're too young. You couldn't keep up with guys our age—you've got sense enough to know that."

"Howie, make him let me go with you." Joey turned away from me. His voice pled with Howie. I think I knew at that minute what the decision would be.

Joey knew what he was doing when he turned to Howie. This was his friend, and he knew it. They had often sat on the school steps during late afternoons in summer when no one was around, and Howie had shown Joey how to pick out a few chords on the banjo. Sometimes he'd ask Joey to sing and he'd make his banjo sing too, and their faces would be all shined up with delight. Howie was kinder to Joey than I was, more patient, more respectful of Joey as an individual.

He looked at me when Joey made his plea. "Why can't he go with us, Josh?"

"He just can't. He wouldn't be able to keep up with us. He'd be a nuisance, and you know it. We've made our plans, Howie, and I think they'll work. But not if we have to have a kid along."

"He can sing," Howie said as if to himself. "He's got a good, clear voice, a little off-pitch now and then, but nice. Lots of people will pay to hear a little kid sing who wouldn't notice older ones. Joey just might do all right for himself."

"I've told you, Howie, he can't go. I won't let him. And that's final."

"Maybe you and me could go it alone, Joey. Let old Josh stay here and boss people around if that's what he likes to do. You and me might get ourselves a lot of loose change if we practiced a little and got into the right spot." He grinned at Joey, and my brother grinned back in triumph. For a minute I was furious with both of them, but even in that minute it struck me that if some

34

artist could paint those two faces, both of them thin from too scanty meals during the past two years, but both of them bright with laughter—if some artist could have caught them at that minute, he could have made a picture that was really something.

So it was settled, and late that night Joey and I crawled out of our room with an old cardboard suitcase full of clothing, the remnants of a tattered blanket, and all the matches I could find. Matches, I felt, were very important. I had read a story somewhere of an expedition that appeared to be all set, everything packed and ready. Then it smashed, all because one little item had been forgotten. No matches. I hunted around and collected every one I could find.

I was too excited to think about how grave a step we were taking. If I thought of Mom and Dad at all, it was with anger which I sought to fan in order to keep up my courage. Nothing mattered except getting away.

We joined Howie, who waited down in our alley with his banjo and a bundle of clothes tucked under his arm. The three of us slept in a park for a few hours that night. Then very early the next morning we found a Salvation Army kitchen open with no one else yet around. A big, tired-looking man shook his head at us, but he gave each of us a bowl of oatmeal. Then he told us not to come back. The food he handed out was for men who must wait in line to get to employment windows—it wasn't for runaway kids.

Our experience that first day showed how right Howie had been in making me allow Joey to come with us. We stopped down on Randolph and Wabash early in the afternoon and tried our luck for the first time at the art of panhandling. That is, Joey and Howie tried it. They were right for it, both of them being small, Joey's blondness contrasting vividly with Howie's great dark eyes and sallow face. I drifted off in the crowd and watched the other two perform.

Joey sang, his small face bright under the blond hair that he had to brush out of his eyes from time to time. His voice was sweet and clear, a little thin, of course, and not always true to pitch, but with Howie covering up for him, he did all right. Howie, with his sense of showmanship, would run his fingers across the strings in a gay arpeggio and then grin up at Joey as if that flurry of notes was some pleasant secret between them. People stopped to watch them. Some smiled as they stood listening, and some sad faces looked sadder than ever. But a lot of people reached out to drop a nickel or a few pennies into Joey's outstretched cap.

They collected seventy-eight cents that afternoon. Then at twilight they joined me, and we moved on in triumph at our beginning. We bought hot dogs and a loaf of bread and still had money enough for some breakfast. We gloated as we ate.

If Joey's singing with Howie's banjo could do that well for us, we were pretty sure that, given the luck to find an available piano, Howie and I could make music that some restaurant owner or dance hall proprietor would pay us to do. Once in a while I'd play popular numbers straight, I thought, and Joey could sing with us. I no longer underestimated Joey. He had done fine that afternoon.

I felt happier than I had felt in weeks. We had found confidence down there on the corner of Randolph and Wabash, seventy-eight cents worth of confidence, and the glow it gave us was a wonderful experience.

When it grew dark, we huddled together under the steps of a stairway leading up to an el platform. We talked softly together for a while, and the words "We can make it; I *know* we can make it" became a refrain. We didn't realize at first how many times we'd repeated those words, and when we did, we carried our refrain to ridiculous lengths and laughed at our own absurdity.

Joey and Howie grew tired very early. They leaned against me for warmth and were soon asleep, but I sat there wide awake for a long time. Little gusts blew scraps of dirty newspaper and flurries of dust into my face from time to time. Overhead the elevated trains rumbled so often that their noise finally became a familiar monotony of which I was barely conscious.

Once a woman came and stood leaning against

the pillar of the stair for a long time. She was so close I could have touched her dress, but she didn't see us. She was crying. She made me think of Kitty, and I was glad when she finally began climbing the steps up to the platform.

Very late in the night when the moonlight made it look like morning, a policeman came by. He stopped to look at us, but after one glance I kept my eyes closed, and he evidently decided to let us sleep. After a long time he walked away, very slowly.

The next morning after a better breakfast than we usually had at home, we started for the freight yards. We had money enough left for streetcar fare, and so, after some inquiries, we found the right car and rode out to the yards in style. We weren't too much concerned about money. We thought we'd ride as far as we could on the freight train; then Howie and Joey could repeat their panhandling stunt, and we could eat until a real job could be located. We had the remainder of the loaf of bread we'd bought the night before; that would have to do us for the train ride.

We found acres of tracks down in the freight yards; I had never known there were so many. We saw trains coming in and leaving, trains being loaded for a run, trains backing, lurching forward, switching—everything was confusion. Adding to that confusion was an army of men, many of them railroad workers; just as many others were loiterers like us. These men were looking around, sizing up the cars and their loads, waiting for the whistles that meant a train was about to start. When that signal came, they would run to leap into a car or swing up on an outer ladder and climb to the top of the train once the wheels had picked up speed.

I asked a cautious question or two whenever I saw a face that looked friendly. There weren't many such. Men's faces seemed to be much alike that year—lean, scowling, and angry. One man who told me that he'd been a hobo for fifteen years was friendly enough, however, and was willing to talk to us. When we told him we were headed west, he didn't question the vagueness of our "west," but pointed out a train and told us it would leave for Iowa that afternoon, would get to Nebraska the next morning. That sounded good to us; that was west and far away from Chicago.

I asked the hobo about the railroad detectives, the bulls of whom I'd heard a lot. Were they really brutal as many of the newspapers and magazine articles described them? Sometimes they were, he told me, especially when the higher-ups began to put on the pressure and a bull felt his job was in danger. He had seen bulls club men off the trains; he'd also seen an angry group of free riders seize a bull and throw him from the train. On the other hand he'd seen riders and bulls sit together for long hours, chatting or playing cards as if everything were all above board and just

39

fine. It all depended, he said; it all depended on your luck.

I asked about the dangers. Yes, he'd seen kids— men too, but mostly kids—get killed if they were careless. Big loads of lumber or steel might shift with a sudden lurch of the train and crush an unwary rider. Some people misjudged the speed of a train and made their grabs for the ladder or the open car too late. Legs were often crushed in accidents of that sort.

A feeling of uneasiness chilled me, uneasiness especially for Joey. He was thin, even to skinniness, and he wasn't as active as most kids his age. He hadn't grown up accustomed to the leaping and climbing and bike riding that I had done as a youngster; he'd had too many years of illness for that. Howie was slender, too, and short, but he was an agile little guy who had survived Chicago's traffic and some of its worst slums. Howie could keep up with me, I was pretty sure, but I was worried about Joey.

I decided against waiting until the freight started. We'd find an open car and hide until we were on our way. If the bulls discovered us and threw us off before we got moving, we'd just have to find another train. I couldn't see Joey undertaking a scramble that was dangerous even for men who had jumped on moving trains for years. Howie agreed with me.

We found an open car filled with big sacks of lime which farmers use to fertilize their fields.

40

There were some fairly good hiding places among these piles, fairly good, that is, if a railroad bull happened to be lax in his car inspection. And, of course, that all depended on your luck. We jumped inside when we felt no one was watching, and in the hour of waiting for the train to start, not a soul came near us. We got to feeling pretty confident after a while, almost as if we had bought tickets for a ride somewhere "out west."

Three men jumped into our car when the train began to pick up speed, but they didn't pay any attention to us. They looked very blue and tired; they didn't even talk to one another.

We rattled out of Chicago, and in an hour or two we were passing farms and small towns; the fields, brown with withered cornstalks, looked ghostly as twilight closed in. We crossed rivers, most of them low and sluggish after the drouth that had burned things up that summer, and then finally we were rushing through nothing but black night with only the light from the engine, at least a mile ahead of our car, to cut the darkness.

Talk lagged that night. All three of us were quiet, a little thoughtful. Once Howie stroked the strings of his banjo a few times, but somehow the chords sounded mournful. I felt as if I couldn't stand to hear them, and I was glad when he shook his head and laid the banjo aside.

Joey had charge of the leftover bread. He took it out after a while, and we cut it up into chunks with Howie's knife. We ate it very slowly, chewing each bite a long time to stretch out the experience of having food in our mouths. Joey finished first and Howie handed him a crust from his own share. "Here, Joey, you eat this. I hate the crusty part," he lied indifferently. That was like Howie.

The rhythmic roar of the wheels soon made us drowsy. There wasn't much to talk about anyway, so we leaned against a high stack of the lime sacks and closed our eyes. Suddenly I remembered what the hobo had said about heavy loads that shifted with a lurching train and sometimes killed riders. I got up and tested the stack above us. It seemed firm as a stone wall. Then I relaxed and went to sleep.

It was toward morning but still dark when a couple railroad bulls came through our car. One of them kicked me in the shins, not hard, but lively enough to let me know he meant business.

"Come on, you kids, you're gettin' off in just about fifteen minutes. You're gettin' off and stayin' off, the whole lousy lot of you."

One of the men over in the corner gave the bulls some lip—didn't hear what he said, but I could tell by the tone.

"We've had our orders, bud, and the company ain't foolin'. This train is crawlin' with free riders tonight. You're gettin' off, brother, and you can wait for the next freight and see what happens."

We got off when the freight stopped. It was cold and dark except for the dim lights around the railroad yards. Down the length of the train we saw men and boys leaping out of car doors or climbing down from the tops of the cars. I thought about frightened rats running out of the path of danger. I didn't like being one of those rats.

I held on to Joey when he made the leap down from the car. He was sleepy and stiff from the cramped position he'd had, and bewildered about what was happening. Howie swore softly, one hand clutching his banjo, the other hand guiding Joey.

There was noise all around us, noise of the panting freight, of the yelling and cursing of angry men as they milled about the train. Suddenly we became aware of another noise, a swelling roar from the town beyond the tracks. We stopped to listen, and in the near-darkness we saw what looked like a wall of men coming toward us. They carried clubs and pitchforks, and as they approached, we could hear the savagery in their voices.

"Don't take another step this way," a huge man yelled, stepping in front of the others. "You can take your empty bellies to another part of the country. We've enough of your kind to feed already. Take another step and we'll club you down like dogs."

There were snarls and yells of rage from our side. A man cried out, "What do you want us to do—throw ourselves under the wheels?" and

43

there was a loud chorus of "Yes! That's right! Do that!"

It was like a horror dream. The thought ran through my mind, "Joey's hearing this. He's only ten, and he's hearing things like this."

Out of the crowd of men the hobo from the Chicago yards was suddenly beside us.

"You boys stay with me. We'll jump the train as soon as it gets movin.' It's all we can do. I'll help the kid on. You two stay close."

And so we waited. It seemed a long time, but finally the signal for pulling out was sounded and the train started moving. Men ran along its side and waited to make their leap. I think the railroad bulls must have given up; they couldn't afford to club men to death because they were stealing another hour's ride.

The hobo lifted Joey like a sack of flour and half-tossed, half-pushed him into an empty car. He yelled to Howie and me, "Stay close. There's a passenger highballin' through town on the other track."

There was, indeed, though I'd been too excited to notice. The light was tearing down the parallel track toward us. It was blinding. I grabbed at the floor of the car and swung up inside. It wasn't hard to do; the freight was still moving slowly.

Howie was right behind me, and I braced myself to help draw him up. But he didn't leap as I expected him to do. He yelled, "Here, catch my banjo, Josh," and as I extended my arms, he
44

leaned back a little and threw the banjo up to me. What happened then, I don't know. I'll never know. But the banjo had no sooner touched my hands than I saw Howie's body lifted by the express train and thrown down the tracks as if it had been an empty crate, a worthless piece of junk.

I had the wildest kind of feeling that I must go after him; it seemed I'd die if I couldn't get to Howie. I heard Joey screaming and a man yelling, "Grab that kid. He's goin' to jump." Then it was as if a dozen pairs of arms grabbed me and threw me down on the floor against the side of the car. I didn't know anything more for a long time.

Chapter Three

Joey and I got off the freight in the late afternoon. The bulls had quieted down after word of the accident traveled through the train, I guess; at least those of us in the car where Joey and I sat saw nothing more of them. We got off the train of our own accord; there was nothing we wanted so much as to get away from that place of tragedy.

It was a small town where we stopped, and no one around the depot paid any attention to us. Joey's face was swollen with his tears, and my legs were shaking until I could hardly walk. We were hungry, but with the numbness of grief, my courage was gone. I couldn't bring myself to face the possibility of a hostile answer if I approached someone for food. I wouldn't have dared to ask for a job. I couldn't have played the finest piano in the country that night; I couldn't have chopped wood or stacked lumber or done any other job even if I had had the chance. I stumbled a time or two when we climbed down from the train, and I held on to Joey's shoulder for support. We walked along the track a little distance and sat down for a while, trying to make some plan for the night.

One of the men who had climbed off the train stopped beside us. He and some of the others had gone into a small store beside the depot and had evidently bought a few groceries. He held a half dozen cans of food in his arms.

"A bunch of us are going to cook a little down the tracks tonight," he said. "If you kids want to come with me, I guess we can spare you a meal."

To refuse the food was plain madness on our part, but when I looked at Joey, he was shaking his head. I felt the same way. We were in too deep a shock for an evening with strangers; we wanted to crawl away with our grief and face it in silence.

I thanked the man and said no, we'd have to be on our way.

"Where's your way?" he asked. "Where are you goin'?"

It was a reasonable question. But I had no answer. I just looked up at him and shook my head.

"I thought so," he said. He took a can of beans and tossed it on the ground at Joey's feet. "Well,

47

good luck, kids. You'd better hitchhike from now on. You'll never be any good on trains after this. And if you want my advice, you better hitchhike home to your folks if you've got any."

He walked off down the tracks without once turning to look back. Joey and I sat there watching him until he disappeared. Then we got up and, leaving the tracks, took off across a field, walking in complete silence but with our hands holding on tightly to one another. Never before had Joey been of so much worth to me as he was on that twilight trek across someone's brown field. I kept thinking, "We're just two now; there's just Joey and me. Get used to it, because Howie is gone. We're just two."

We came finally to a ravine that cut through the field and to a footbridge that crossed the big ditch which was dry now, with a carpet of grass and weeds on its floor. The depth of the ravine afforded protection from the chilly wind, a wind that was sharper than it had been the night before in Chicago.

We threw our clothes and blankets and Howie's banjo on a pile of leaves and sat down to rest. It was dark by that time, and the stillness out in that field was immense and terribly lonely. And then, worse than the stillness, came the faraway whistle of a train and the rumble of cars. A stab of agony went through me. I wondered if I would ever again be able to hear the noises of a train without hurting at the memory of Howie.

48

That night under the bridge, Joey and I cried together. It was the first time I had cried since I was a very small boy; there had always been a stubborn streak in me that refused to allow tears no matter how much I had been hurt. Not that night in the ravine.

Finally I made myself face the situation. I opened the can of beans with my knife and divided them between us. "We'll eat, Joey, and then we'll think things through."

We felt a great deal better after we had eaten. The tramp-man's gift restored some of the energy which fatigue and terror had drained from us. We leaned against the bank of the ravine and talked quietly together.

"Do you want to go home, Joey?" I asked. "Because if you do, I'll hitchhike back with you and then strike out on my own."

"You wouldn't go home even if we got back to Chicago, would you?" Joey asked.

I thought of Dad's face, of his anger. I pictured the contempt he'd have for my brief running away. I remembered Mom saying maybe it was best that I leave.

"I think I'd rather starve. I don't want to starve, but it would be better than going back home. They won't scold you, Joey; they'll be glad to have you back. But me—I think I'll take the chance on my own."

Joey nodded. "I think I'll take the chance with you," he said.

I didn't tell him that I was glad, but I was; deeply, gratefully glad. I said, "It's going to be harder for us to find a job without—without Howie. It's going to be rough. But maybe—"

There was still a maybe, still a thin hope. We had been so sure, so confident only twenty-four hours earlier. The future had looked so good as the three of us laughed under the el platform the night before.

We slept for a while, a troubled, restless sleep for me. It grew cold during the night, and toward morning we were awakened by a chill rain blowing in our faces. I got out an extra jacket for Joey and helped him to overcome the stiffness in his arms so that he could get into it.

We picked up our belongings and trudged through the wet meadow, hungry and still numb with our grief. I wanted to get to a town, some place where there was a soup kitchen and maybe a chance of getting the job Howie and I had hoped to find. The memory, though, of that army of men meeting the train only a few hours before made me feel weak with despair. I wondered if there were any place in the world where Joey and I would be welcome.

Just a chance, I kept thinking, just one chance to dig a ditch or clean a cesspool—I wouldn't ask to play a piano—just a chance to earn enough money for two good breakfasts.

We didn't find a town that morning, but toward noon we came upon a ramshackle farmhouse, about as dreary a place as I had ever seen, even in the slum area where Howie had lived. The yard around it was hard-packed clay, and it was cluttered with all kinds of debris: piles of rotting boards, cracked dishes, some cast-off toys, broken-down chairs and other pieces of furniture. The only sign of life was a listless-looking white rooster which watched us indifferently for a minute and then took off on his long yellow legs. I had an idea that people as needy as we were had left this place, maybe with big plans, maybe telling themselves they knew they could make it.

We went inside and made a quick inspection. Nothing there. Nothing, that is, except a rusty old kitchen range, and that was a welcome sight.

We gathered wood and old papers from the yard, and in a few minutes we had a fire going that warmed our bodies and cheered our hearts. Joey almost embraced that stove for a while as his clothing dried. Gradually, the blueness left his lips, and he smiled at me. "Smells great, doesn't it, Josh?" he asked, pointing to the smoke that swirled around the lids of the stove. It did. It smelled friendly and warm. It comforted the aching for Howie.

I went outside after a time, thinking maybe there might be a kitchen garden somewhere, that there might possibly be an overlooked hill of potatoes or a turnip or two. It was likely that people had been living there during the summer because their rooster was still roaming the place. Finally I

51

did find a fenced-in lot that had evidently been a garden, but there were no overlooked potatoes or turnips in it. Nothing but weeds and crabgrass. Whoever lived there had made a clean sweep of everything edible. Everything, it suddenly occured to me, except the white rooster.

He was curious, that old fellow. He had come back to the yard and was studying me, cautiously, though, as if he sensed danger in the air. And truly there was danger for him at that minute, for I had a sudden vivid and ravenous vision of a boiled chicken dinner.

I made a dash for him, and he ran for his life. Neither of us was feeling too well that morning, but we were both desperate. We circled the house a couple of times with all the speed we could muster; finally he came to grief when he got tangled up in a mass of wire that had been thrown over the fence. I caught him there, and I felt a glow of elation that Joey and I would have food for the next several meals.

It took a long time to get our rooster ready for cooking. We found an old bucket in which we heated water to help remove the feathers. The same bucket had to be washed out and serve as a cooking kettle when I had at last done a pretty good job of getting the feathers removed. While I worked, Joey explored the heap of debris outside, finding a cracked china cup and a real treasure in the form of an old salt shaker with a packed and soggy mass of salt in the bottom. We dissolved the salt in hot water and saved the liquid to flavor our meat when it was done.

That rooster was, without doubt, one of the toughest fowls that had ever been hatched. We boiled it the rest of the day, testing it with our knife from time to time and finding the flesh just as tough and unyielding at twilight as it had been at noon.

The broth was pretty good, though; we took turns drinking it from the cracked cup, and though it wasn't the best soup I'd ever tasted, it wasn't too bad. The liver at least became tender after a few hours of cooking, and our rooster had a remarkably fine liver; I made Joey eat it while we waited hopefully for the rest of the meat to get done.

We enjoyed our meal, poor as it was, and that night as a cold rain pelted against the windows, we knew the wonderful security of a roof and a fire. It wasn't our roof, of course, and I half expected that at any minute someone would appear and order us to be off. But such a time would have to be met when it came. For that hour of gathering darkness with the silence of the prairies all about us, I gave myself up to the warmth of the stove and the comfort of a pallet made of our blanket with our jackets rolled up for pillows.

Joey was soon asleep. I lay for a long time watching the trembling shadows which the light from the stove threw upon the ceiling. It occurred to me that in a nation of hungry people, I was

almost as small and helpless as Joey. I knew that
both he and I could be wiped out as quickly as
Howie had been, and that very few people would
ever know or care. I knew just as well, though,
that Joey and I were going to tackle the days
ahead of us together. We had lost Howie and the
shock was still inside us; the knowledge that we
were crippled without him was frightening. Still,
we were not going home to eat food that Mom
had bought with a day of ironing; I was not going
to eat food that Dad would resent my swallowing.

I sat up for a while and looked down at my
brother, wondering at the callous indifference I
had so often felt toward him. That night I knew
that the small boy stretched out on our makeshift
bed was all I had in the world to make me feel a
part of the human race. I leaned over as I had
that last morning at home and tucked the blanket
more carefully around his shoulders; he stirred a
little in his sleep, moving closer to me, and when I
finally slept, I was comforted by Joey's presence.

We heated up more chicken broth the next
morning for breakfast, and as we were taking
turns at drinking from the cracked cup, I saw a
man and woman coming toward the house. I
braced myself for trouble and went to the door.
Joey stood close at my side.

"Makin' yourself at home, I see," said the man
as he came up to the porch. "How many are you
here?"

"Just us two. I'm Josh Grondowski—this is my

54

brother. We were wet and cold so we spent the night here. We haven't hurt anything."

The woman said, "Why, it's just two boys, Ben, just two young boys." She smiled at us. I don't know whether I smiled at her or not, but Joey did, his friendliest smile, and you could see the woman liked him right away.

The man wasn't so quick to be friendly. "Runaways, I suppose?"

I shrugged. "There wasn't enough to eat at home. We're on our way to our grandfather's in Montana. He asked us to come." The lie about a grandfather seemed a good thing in case this man wanted to make trouble. I doubted if he cared, though. He looked as if he had too many troubles of his own to care much about whether two kids were runaways or not.

"Well, I can imagine the old man's real happy. Two more mouths to feed makes most of us feel privileged and cheerful these days," he said sourly. "How you goin' to manage to eat till you get there?"

"I play the piano pretty well—I've been hoping maybe I could find a job—I play pretty well," I repeated, worried and unsure. The man's face convinced me that I had said a ridiculous thing.

"So you want a job at playin' the piano?"

"That's what—it's what I'd hoped," I said.

"Well, young man, let me tell you somethin'. You got as much chance of findin' a job like that around here as a snowball's got of stayin' hard in

Hades. In fact, you got as much chance of findin' *any* job at all as that snowball's got."

I didn't answer. The man was making me realize that every fear of mine was real. His words were hard to take, but I knew that he was only honest. He probably hated that kind of honesty as much as I did.

"Where you from?" he asked after a minute.

"Chicago," I answered. "We just got into this part of the country night before last."

"Well, get on to your grandpa's or back to Chicago—whichever is closest. You're in a desperate part of the country here. We're broke. We're broke flat. This house and stove belong to me—tenants moved out last week—and the whole danged place ain't worth thirty cents. Not with the stove throwed in."

"We were sure glad to stay here last night," I said.

"Have you had anything to eat?" the woman asked. Her eyes were kind. She was looking at Joey.

I knew there might be trouble over the rooster, but I supposed I'd have to face it. "We found a chicken, ma'am, and I cooked it. I hope it wasn't yours?"

She shook her head. "No, we sold most of what we had. I cooked the rest and canned them. No use keeping chickens. Eggs ain't worth the gas it takes to get 'em to town. No, I reckon that must have been one of the chickens the Helmses left behind. A right middle-aged one, I'll bet."

I showed her our boiled chicken, and she poked it with her finger. "I'll put it through the meat grinder. It won't help much, but maybe we can get a little nourish out of it. You boys can come on up for dinner."

"Josie," the man said sternly.

"We can give them *one* meal, Ben. You're right in tellin' them to head for their folks, but we're goin' to give them one meal. Biscuits and molasses and maybe something or other I can fix up out of this chicken. I guess we can share a meal with two boys."

"Maybe we shouldn't," I said. "Joey and I don't want to take food you need."

It was the man who answered me. "No, come on up to the house. A biscuit or two won't send us downhill much faster than we're goin' now. It's just that Josie wants to feed every hungry man who comes to the door. That's got to stop—but like she says, we can share with two boys."

And so we went with them up the road to their place, which wasn't a lot better than the one we had left except there was a little furniture in the house. There was a shabby old rug on the living room floor, a few chairs, and a rickety-looking table holding a pile of newspapers and a few faded photographs. There was a little framed card on the wall with birds and flowers on it and the name of some Nebraska town in gold letters; there was also a picture of the presidential candidate Franklin Roosevelt, which had been cut from a newspaper and pinned under an old-fashioned clock.

The woman went immediately to the kitchen where she began fixing something for dinner. Joey and I sat in the living room and listened to the man as he talked on and on of the hard times that were with us and the harder times we might expect later on.

He jerked his finger toward the newspaper picture on the wall. "Now that fellow—Josie puts some stock in what he says. Not me. Maybe he's got some new ideas—more than likely it's just hot air. Things have gone too far. I don't think him nor anybody else can do anything now. We're beat! We'd just as well give up and—"

"Ben," the woman called from the kitchen, "they're just boys. Can't you talk of something a little more cheerful? We don't help ourselves with all this carryin' on."

If he heard her, he paid no attention. "Last hog I took to market was a big one," he continued as if the woman hadn't spoken. "Upwards of two-fifty it weighed. You know what I got for it? After shipping and yard expenses, exactly ninety-eight cents. That's what I got for it. Ninety-eight cents. And I had to take it—I had to take what I could get because I hadn't any feed for it. I'd ha' had a dead critter on my hands so I took the ninety-eight cents." He had been handling a folded newspaper nervously as he talked, and now he threw it on the table with a gesture of disgust. "This is the kind of country you boys are in—a flat broke country that's growin' flatter broke. Banks have already foreclosed on half the farms in this county. Mine'll go in matter of months—everything we've worked for will be up on the auction block."

Joey and I didn't say anything. We didn't know what to say. This angry, hopeless talk was so much like Dad's that it made me feel restless and uneasy. I don't think, though, that the man expected us to say anything; he didn't even care whether we were listening or not. He just had to talk.

He was starting in again about more troubles of the times when the woman came and stood at the door. "Ben, I want you to hush now, and get washed up for dinner," she said quietly. "You boys can make good use of a pan of water, too. Now, come on, all of you, and get ready for a bite to eat."

It was a good dinner. There were plenty of biscuits, and the woman kept asking us to eat more. She managed the conversation all during the meal, and I could see that she was determined to keep her husband off the subject of his hardships.

When we had finished eating, she pointed to Howie's banjo lying on our jackets, and asked if I could play it. I had been dreading the first time that I would have to hear those strings again, but

I knew that reality had to be faced. I didn't have Howie's skill on the banjo by a long way, but I twanged a few chords and asked Joey to sing. It was a hard moment for both of us, but it pleased the couple who sat listening. I noticed that as the man watched Joey sing, his face grew quieter and less angry-looking. After a while he laid his arm on the back of his wife's chair, and his hand touched her shoulder. When Joey grew tired, they thanked him, and before we left, the man gave him a bag containing a half dozen large potatoes.

"These will help out for a few meals," he said. He shook hands with us. The woman hugged Joey.

Then we were out on the road again. We got a ride from a farmer, a cheerful man whose friendliness reassured us, helped us to forget the crowd of men in a town not many miles away, men who had met us in the middle of the night with pitchforks. Our spirits rose on that ride. We had had a sheltered night and kindness from the couple we'd just left; we had a bag of potatoes and now a lift of several miles from a man who told us in a pleasant drawl that he guessed we'd find work of some kind or other in the next town. Times were bad, yes, he said, but he reckoned that times had been bad, off and on, for many a year and somehow people had managed to get by. He thought that two boys like us would get along all right, especially if we weren't afraid of hard work and low wages. It was good to find someone with a little hope. I told him so when he stopped the car to let us out and showed us the road to take into town.

After walking a mile or two, we decided that we wouldn't go into town that evening, that we'd camp out and go in the next morning when we were rested and fresh. Actually, we dreaded the town in spite of the farmer's reassurance—at least, I did. The angry snarls of the men in the railroad yards came back to my ears at the thought of a town. Anyway, the rain had stopped and the night was much warmer than the one before; a night in the woods would not be too uncomfortable, and it would delay for a while the facing of strangers in a town.

We had eaten one good meal that day, and it seemed extravagant to give ourselves the luxury of a baked potato that night. Still, we felt rich in having so much food, and since our hunger was never quite satisfied, we gave ourselves a treat, though we limited our meal to one potato to be shared rather than one each which we would have liked.

I dug a shallow trench and built a fire in it. Then Joey and I sat watching the fire burn down to a bed of blue and rosy coals, talking quietly together as we waited for our potato to bake. When the darkness grew deeper, our fire glowed with a radiance that made a little island of light in the night. A few spirals of smoke drifted upward occasionally as Joey added a pile of twigs or clump of leaves to the coals.

We felt perfectly safe there in the quiet woods with the beauty of our fire, the good smell of our roasting potato, and the comfort of being together. We didn't dream of danger, not even when we heard someone approaching, and the attack, when it came, filled us with as much amazement as it did fear.

Four or five boys were in the group that suddenly leaped upon us, big fellows with shaggy hair and harsh, high voices. They screamed at us, but I understood only part of what they said—just enough to know that they were hungry.

Joey had had no dealings with thugs or hoodlums; he made the mistake of holding on to the bag of potatoes as fiercely as if he stood a chance against those boys who were almost men. One of the attackers knocked him flat, and when I ran to his rescue, all four or five of them took out their venom on me, enraged, I guess, at anyone who had a bite to eat while they starved.

They left us after a few minutes, taking with them Joey's bag of potatoes and the baked potato too, which they raked out of the ashes. They took our blanket and our extra clothes; one of them picked up Howie's banjo, looked at it a moment, and then for some unexplained reason, threw it contemptuously back on the ground.

When they were gone, we dragged ourselves together and started out for the highway. Joey was more frightened than physically hurt, but my forehead was bleeding from a deep cut and my eyes were almost swollen shut. When we got into town, a policeman bawled me out for fighting. He didn't make us get out of town, though. He even let us sleep in the jail that night.

Chapter Four

I noticed after a few weeks that I was thinking of nothing but food. Even the hopes of finding a job dwindled to the point of being extinguished altogether. But the question of the next meal was always with me, pressing and immediate.

There had been many other interests in previous years; even in the midst of very difficult months at home there had been time for other interests. There had always been the dream of playing in an orchestra, dreams of the recitals which I would one day give, of the praise and acclaim my art would inspire. With Howie I had sometimes planned to run away, to roam the world (always with money in our pockets), to see sights and have adventures and come back heroes. There had been sports and school and teachers, good and bad; there had been books and an occasional movie where we always watched each feature twice at least. There had been girls, which was a secret interest, but a very real one. I often wondered about girls, at their soft prettiness, their grace, their capricious little ways. Sometimes I had stared at the mass of bright curls belonging to the girl who sat at the desk in front of me, and new music had come into my mind, gentle, whispering music that a boy with the solemn name of Josh Grondowski might sometime play for the girl he loved.

Not anymore. There were no dreams now, no hopes, no interests except in finding food enough to keep Joey and me alive. Sometimes we'd get a bowl of dishwatery broth at a soup kitchen and we'd be told, "Just one meal. One meal is all we have for tramp-kids. We've got our own to feed." And then we'd hide out in a doorway or a railroad depot or a city park, and the little sleep I'd get would be troubled with the problem of where to find a bite of breakfast, how to go about the business of searching or begging or stealing.

We almost starved before I went to the garbage cans. I'd read in the papers back home of people doing that; I didn't believe I could ever bring myself to it. But I did. I made Joey stay inside a warm doorway, and I went around to an alley back of a restaurant. There were two men and a woman pawing through the cans. There were rats

65

too. The rats were brazen enough, but we four humans tried to ignore the presence of one another. I found some frozen bread and two steak bones with a little meat still on them. I washed the bones in the lavatory of a public rest room; then Joey and I found a sheltered place in a vacant lot where we built a fire and warmed the food. Joey ate it gratefully, but each bite sickened me as I remembered the garbage cans and the rats and the shamed people who couldn't look at one another. I swore I'd never go back for that kind of food again, but I did, many times. I had to do it. One thing I was proud of, though: I never allowed Joey to go with me. Never.

But I had reason to feel ashamed on another score. I turned coward when it became necessary for us to beg. The humiliation of begging was as hard for me to bear as hunger, and it left deeper scars. And though I spared Joey the indignity of the garbage cans, I *did* let him take over the hateful business of going from door to door.

Joey never complained; he assumed that begging was his role rather than mine. "It's better for *me* to do the asking, Josh. I'm younger and they'll give to little kids where they won't give a scrap to big guys."

He was right, of course. People would look at his thin face with the big shadowy eyes, and they'd share whatever they had with him. He was often casual about the reaction of people to him. "The lady cried—I guess she was real sorry for me," he told me indifferently one night as he spread out his gift of bread and an apple. Once he was given an old sweater; another time a warm cap. People found it hard, I think, to turn Joey from their doors.

Begging was, indeed, much more effective with Joey doing the job, but I finally realized that I was hiding like a scared rabbit and allowing a ten-year-old boy to face the humility because I didn't like it. After that I did my share. It was terrible, and I never became accustomed to it. However, night after night Joey and I started out, sometimes taking alternate houses, sometimes trying our luck on separate blocks.

One night a girl came to the kitchen door when I knocked. I had a fleeting impression that she was very pretty. I don't really know what she was like, for after that first glance I couldn't look at her again. I looked past her and muttered, "I hate to say this—but I'm hungry."

Her voice was nice. I heard her say, "It's a boy who's hungry, Daddy. May I give him something?"

A tall man came to the door and looked at me. "Yes, Betsy, by all means. Give him some of our roast," he said, and then he walked away.

In a few minutes she came back to the door with a little cardboard box containing food that smelled wonderful. I wanted to look into her eyes and thank her, but I couldn't. I took the box and just stood there for a few seconds, hurting because I was forced to beg, to stand before her deprived of confidence.

The girl spoke to me then in a very low voice. She said, "I hope things will be better for you soon. I feel so ashamed that I have food when the times force boys like you to go hungry."

I'll never know her name, and I'll never know if she was really as pretty as that first glance told me she was. I know only one thing about her, and that was the fact that she fed my hungry stomach and laid a kind of healing balm on a part of my spirit that was raw with the beating it was taking.

There were many times when I was ready to give up during the cold weeks of November, times when I really believed that Joey and I would have to wander out into some open field and let the cold finish us off. But always at such times something turned up, something happened which seemed to say "Not yet, not yet," and we would find food and rest and the spirit to go on.

It was like that the night we stopped at a tiny farmhouse somewhere in Nebraska, and a very old lady asked us to come inside. She gave us supper at a little table in the kitchen where a good fire burned and a kettle poured out steam from its copper spout.

She watched us thoughtfully while we ate. "Do you smoke?" she asked me after a while.

If there had been any laughter in me, I would have considered that a joke. "Ma'am, if I had the money to buy cigarettes, I'd have bought something for us to eat instead of asking you." I said.

She nodded. "All right then. You boys can stay the night here. I had to ask about smoking because I'm fearful of fire. But you can stay." She paused a minute. "I think you'll have to take a bath, though, and after you're in bed, I'll wash your clothes."

A bath. I wondered if she knew what that meant to us. Joey and I washed with soap and hot water for the first time since we had left home. Our bodies were clean and refreshed and respectable in the suits of long underwear which the woman told us had once belonged to her husband. We lay in a soft bed that night under a feather comforter; we moaned a little before we slept, half in weariness, half in the wonder of being comfortable, and we refused to think of another day.

The lady let us sleep until almost noon the next day. Then she came in softly and laid our clothes, freshly washed and ironed, on the foot of the bed. She stood there looking down at us.

"Poor little fellows, you were dead tired, weren't you?" she said. She raised the shades at the windows and then walked to the door. "Better get up and into your clean clothes now. I've a good breakfast for you. Maybe the sleep and food will give you strength to get to wherever you're going."

She had wonderful food for us—hot cereal and

toast and cocoa. When I had eaten, I couldn't believe how well I felt, how strong a surge of confidence built up inside me.

The woman wanted to know any number of things about us. "Do you have any parents?" she asked me.

She was kind and good. I didn't want to be rude, but I began to feel wary and uneasy. I was silent for so long that she repeated her question. "I suppose so," I answered. Then, ashamed, I said, "Yes—yes, we have."

"Do they know where you are?"

"I don't think so, ma'am."

"You ran away, didn't you?"

"No, ma'am. They knew we were leaving. At least, my mother knew that *I* was leaving. Joey decided to come with me at the last minute."

"Were you in trouble?"

"Yes, ma'am. Too big an appetite."

She shook her head and drew a deep breath. "They must be suffering these days," she said after a long pause.

I didn't answer. The woman sat looking at us, frowning a little.

After a while she went to a table, and from the drawer beneath it she took out paper and envelopes and stamps. Then she beckoned me to come to the table.

"Now, write something to Mama," she said, putting a hand on my shoulder.

"I'm sorry, ma'am; I can't," I told her.

"You can write, can't you? You know how to read and write, don't you?"

Her question made me mad. I had been an honor student in high school. "Yes," I answered, "I know how to read and write. But I can't. At least I—I just won't."

"You have a hard nature, little man," she said quietly.

"I suppose you're right. I hate to be mean after what you've done for us. I don't want to be mean. But I don't think you can understand. There's just nothing I can say to my folks. Nothing. If Joey wants to write, he can."

She turned to my brother. "How about it, Joey?"

"Yes," he said, "I'll write a note to them. But I can't say I'm coming home. Josh and I are going to stick together."

"Well, then, that's the way it is. Anyway your mama is going to sleep better knowing that you're still alive."

Joey showed me what he had written. He told our parents that we were in Nebraska, that we were well and getting along just fine. They were not to worry, and he would try to send them a line once in a while. That was all. His letter really told them nothing of what we were living through; still, as the old woman said, it at least let them know that we were still alive. She gave Joey some stamped envelopes and made him promise that he'd write whenever he could.

We left that little house regretfully in the early afternoon. We had found cleanliness and rest as well as nourishing food in amounts that satisfied our huge appetites. We wished that we could stay with her, but we knew the rules: one night, one meal. Two meals at the most. After that we must move on. It was understandable. There was no reason why any charity or any person should look after us. We were on our own, and for people on their own, it was a one-night stand unless, by some chance, they had some money in their pockets.

We seemed to be in a cycle of good luck, for we had gone no more than three or four miles down the highway when a truck passed us, its big tires humming along the concrete. The driver threw up his hand as he passed us, and we gave him the hitchhiker's gesture without really hoping that he might stop. Then we saw the speed slacken and the big truck edge over on the shoulder of the road. We ran toward it, hardly believing our good luck.

The driver was a thin, dark man with a tired look in his eyes. He smiled at us, a little wearily I thought, and he spoke in a kind of dry, toneless voice.

"Where to?" he asked.

"We're just moving along. We'll go anywhere."

He didn't seem surprised. There were plenty of people just moving along these days. "You from around here?" he asked.

"No. Chicago. We've been on the road since the first of October."

"No folks?"

"No, we're on our own."

He seemed to be studying us. Finally he said, "I'm taking this load down to New Orleans. You want to go south?"

It was a bitterly cold day. I could have cheered at the thought of getting to a warm climate. "Would you take us? I'll help in any way I can."

"Do you have any money?"

"Not a cent." I expected this would end the deal. No money for food and room, no money to pay for the ride. I braced myself for a "Nothing doing, kid," but I was in for a surprise.

"Well, I've been broke quite a few times myself—I know how it feels. Give the youngster a hand and climb in."

The truck cab was warm, and the comfort of riding was a joy to our tired legs. After he'd asked us our names, the man looked straight ahead of him as he drove, and for miles he didn't say a word. The drone of the wheels made Joey drowsy, and he dropped off to sleep, leaning against my shoulder. The man glanced at him once, and I noticed a kind of half-smile on his lips.

"Pretty young for a jaunt like this, isn't he?" he asked, turning to look at me for a second.

"Yes, he's only ten, but he was set on coming with me."

He talked to me a little after that—asked

where we had been and how we had managed to stay alive. He would acknowledge something I'd say with a nod occasionally, but I had the feeling that he was giving most of his attention to the road and his driving.

After we'd traveled about three hours, we drew over onto the shoulder again. "Have to rest a little," the man said. "Long straight slab gets you hypnotized after a while." When he got out of the cab, I followed him and let Joey go on sleeping. The man leaned against a front wheel and rolled a cigarette quickly and carelessly as if he'd done it for a long time. "What was the trouble about?" he asked curtly as if he were sure I knew what he was talking about.

I supposed he meant the trouble at home, but I just looked dumb and didn't answer.

"You know what I mean. Why did you run away?"

I hesitated. The things that had happened at home shamed me. I had grown up believing that only ne'er-do-wells lacked food, that only people in homes of low standards shouted insults at one another, begrudged the food that others swallowed. Now Joey and I were from such a home. The music and laughter and love that had once been part of our lives had been hopelessly shattered. I looked up at the man standing before me. "I hate to talk about it," I said in a low voice.

"You don't have to, I suppose, but before we get too far, I'd like to know something more about the boys I'm hauling south. I don't want the police on my neck for helping two runaways. Now why'd you tell me you had no folks—that isn't the case, is it?"

I stared at the ground for a minute. Then I opened up and told him everything that had happened between Dad and me, how things had been going from bad to worse, how Mom had even agreed that it would be better for me to clear out.

He had a way of sighing deeply as if there were some heaviness in his chest. He ground out his cigarette as he sighed and made no comment on what I had told him. I got the impression that he wanted to change the subject.

"How old are you, Josh?" he asked abruptly.

"Fifteen."

He nodded. "I thought so. What month were you born?"

It struck me as being strange that on a cold day in winter when half of the world was starving, this man would care about my birthday. It was none of my business, though, so I answered as if it were a perfectly natural question. "June—June twelfth."

He took off his hat and pushed a lock of black hair back from his forehead. "That's pretty close," he said. "My kid was born in April of that year. His name was David."

"He died?" I asked, and then wished that I hadn't.

"Yes. He died. Five years ago. He was about as

tall as Joey—heavier, though, and brown as a little Indian. Looking at you makes me realize how big he would have been. Well"—he turned and opened the door of the cab—"we'd better get on down the road. We've got a lot of miles ahead of us."

The three of us were very quiet during the long afternoon. Joey slept quite a lot, but even when he woke, he sat with his hands clasped over the old banjo and said nothing. The man seemed to have something on his mind, and I, feeling rested and relaxed, gave myself up to a daydream of warm southern skies, of a job, of a place where life would be a little kinder.

It began to snow hard in late afternoon. At dusk we drew up in front of a small cafe beside the road. The light from the windows barely showed through the swirling snowflakes outside.

"We'd better have something to eat," the driver said as we stopped. He jumped down and held up his arms to help Joey down from the cab. He laughed a little as he tousled Joey's hair, and there was a friendliness in his manner that made me feel I could trust him.

I was worried, though, about the matter of eating. "A lady gave Joey and me a good breakfast this morning," I told him. "We can get along on one meal a day."

"No, come on in," he said, starting up the path toward the door.

"I don't have a cent." I thought maybe he had forgotten.

"You told me that. We're not going to have steak. Just soup and hamburgers. Come on."

They knew him at the cafe. The waitress called him Lonnie, and the man who was frying hamburgers in the kitchen stuck his head around the corner and talked to him.

"See you got friends with you," he said.

"Yes. Couple guys from the Windy City. Going down to Louisiana with me."

As we sat at the counter waiting for our food, he talked and joked, sometimes with us, sometimes with the cook and the waitress. When Joey addressed him as Mister, he told us to call him Lonnie. "That's what my niece calls me," he said. "I tell her she might show me a little respect and put 'Uncle' in front of my name, but she's nearly fourteen and pretty set in her ways."

Then he asked Joey about the banjo, if he could play it and so on. Little by little we told him about Howie, about our plans to find a place where I could play piano and where maybe Joey could accompany me with the banjo when he learned to play better.

Lonnie seemed interested. He kept looking at me while we talked as if he were thinking of something. When the waitress came to wipe off the counter in front of us, he said, "Bessie, is that old piano still in the next room?" He jerked his head toward an adjoining room that looked like a makeshift dining room.

"Sure," the woman said. "You buyin' up junk on this trip?"

"This kid says he can play. I want to hear him. All right if we go in while the hamburgers are cooking?"

"Come on." She motioned for me to follow her, and led the way into the next room. "This ain't no Steinway, but you're welcome to try it," she said.

The empty little dining room was cold, and the piano was pretty close to being the junk the waitress had called it. Some two months had passed since I had even seen a piano, and this one, junk though it might be, looked good to me. My fingers felt stiff at first, and it took me a little while to get going. It wasn't long, though, until I began to feel at home again, almost as if Howie were beside me and Miss Crowne were listening from her office. My confidence began to return, and I played for Lonnie and the waitress, the cook and two or three customers with all the skill I could rediscover, with all the spirit left in me.

As music it wasn't very much, but they liked it. They had all crowded inside the door and had stood there in the cold, listening while I played. They clapped when I was through, and they said that surely there must be a job someplace for a kid who could play like that. Joey was beaming. I could see that he felt our troubles were almost over.

While we were eating, the waitress came over and gave Lonnie a slip of paper with a name and address written on it. "Lonnie, this man, Pete Harris, is a cousin of mine," she explained. "He grew up here in Nebraska; we went to school together. He's been down South for fifteen, maybe twenty years now, but he always keeps in touch. Reason I'm tellin' you this is that Pete has a carnival down near Baton Rouge—not much of a carnival, I guess. He's operatin' on a shoestring, he told us, but I know he hires piano players sometimes. He might, he just might, have a place for this boy. Will you be anywhere near Baton Rouge on your way down?"

"I can make it a point to be there," Lonnie answered.

"Pete's a pretty good sort of fellow. He'll go out of his way to help someone down on his luck; I've got reason to know that. He's always been a showman; even when he was a kid, he was forever puttin' on some kind of show. That's been his life, and that's all he'll ever do. He'll never get rich at it, though; he's the sort of guy who looks after the other fellow before himself."

"Not many of that breed left," Lonnie said thoughtfully.

"You're plenty right there ain't. Now, of course, I don't know Pete's circumstances, but I know that if he has a place or can make one for this boy, he'll do it." She nodded at me. "Tell him

79

Bessie Jenkins recommended you—he'll like doin' me a favor."

The waitress was not a pretty woman, and her voice was not as pleasant as I liked women's voices to be, but she looked and sounded wonderful to me that snowy evening. I tried to tell her how much I appreciated her interest in me.

We slept in the back of the truck that night, wedged in between the big cartons packed there, but well wrapped in the blankets Lonnie carried with him. Cold and hunger had kept me awake many times, but this night it was excitement that kept sleep from me. I stared up in the darkness for hour after hour and tried to think of the future. Nothing was very clear—my goal was vague and undefined. I guess the possibility for survival was all I asked.

I thought the other two were sound asleep, but after a long time Lonnie's voice came out of the dark from the other side of the truck. He seemed to know that I was awake.

"You don't forgive easily, do you, Josh?"

I knew he was thinking of Dad. "No," I said, "I guess I don't."

"Haven't you ever made any mistakes yourself?"

"Of course."

"But you somehow got the idea that men have no right to make mistakes? That it's just a privilege of kids?"

I didn't answer. He was quiet for a long time,

and I thought he wasn't going to say anything more which was all right with me. After a while, however, he spoke again.

"Everyone makes mistakes. I made one once, and it's nearly driven me out of my mind at times. My boy—I told you he died five years ago—well, he complained of a bad bellyache one night. His mother wanted to call a doctor, but I thought that it was just a case of a kid eating a little too much or getting hold of something that didn't agree with him. I made him take a big dose of castor oil. My mother had given me that remedy many a time, and I'd always gotten better in a few hours. But it wasn't right for Davy. He had appendicitis. It killed him."

It wasn't easy to find words. I tried to tell him I was sorry, but I stumbled miserably. I don't think he was paying much attention to what I said anyway. He kind of muttered the next words to himself. He said, "If I met your dad tonight, I'd shake hands with him. And I'd say, 'Brother, I know just how you feel.'"

I could hear him turn so that he was facing the outside of the truck. Neither of us said anything more.

Chapter Five

Lonnie became more and more our friend as the days and long evenings passed. He talked a lot about the possibility of my finding a job. "If this Pete Harris doesn't come through with work for you, we'll see if we can't hit someone else. I know some people down in New Orleans who may be able to give us a lead. Folks are great for music down there—I think we have a pretty good chance of finding something for you."

When I stopped to think about it, I was surprised at how much I needed the confidence and assurance that Lonnie gave us. I had considered myself pretty well grown up; I was proud that in spite of our hardships I had been able to take care of Joey, had been able to find food to sustain his life and mine. Now, all at once I was conscious of a sense of security that had not been mine since we left home and for many months before; the confidence of having an adult take the position of a father. Not only was the pinch of winter leaving our bodies, allowing us to relax as we left the snow and icy roads of Nebraska, but the worries and tensions that had plagued every waking moment were leaving our minds. All at once, Joey at ten and I at fifteen, had the right to be boys again. It was Lonnie who made the correct turns on the long road; it was Lonnie who was taking the responsibility of finding Pete Harris and the carnival for us; it was Lonnie who said, "Toast and three eggs, over easy, please. Milk for the boys, coffee for me," when we stopped for breakfast, a decently cooked breakfast unspoiled by begging.

I had not, however, sluffed off all responsibility. On a crumpled piece of paper I carefully set down the amount of money which Lonnie paid for our food at each meal. He asked me once what I was doing, and I told him.

"I'm not worried over the cost of an egg or two and a few hamburgers, Josh," he said.

"I know you're not. But I'll feel better if I can get a job and pay you back for what you're spending on us."

He agreed with me. "I think maybe you're right," he said. "Don't feel you're being pressed, though. Take care of the kid before you start sending money to me."

I liked the way he spoke of my sending money as if the probability of my getting a job and earning money to pay my debts was a very real one. It was a boost to my wavering optimism.

The first day that we hit warm weather we were on a road down in Texas close to the Arkansas border. Lonnie bought bread and cheese and a bottle of milk, and we ate our noon meal on the grass under a clump of trees. Joey breathed great lungfuls of the soft air with delight; he and Lonnie ran together up the road and back, laughing and panting as they sat down to the picnic lunch I had spread out beside the truck.

When we had eaten, Joey practiced a little on the banjo and Lonnie sang a few songs that were currently being heard on the radio, encouraging Joey to find the right chords for an accompaniment. I listened to them for a while, and then, being well-fed and comfortable in the warm air, I hid my face in the grass and went to sleep.

When I awoke, they were talking quietly together, evidently about me. I heard Lonnie say, "So, I take it you're pretty fond of your big brother, aren't you?"

I think Joey was slightly embarrassed. We never talked much about such things. We left that sort of talk for Kitty and Mom.

Joey hesitated a little. "Yes, I like him. I like him a lot."

"I have an idea your dad is thinking a lot about you boys these days."

Joey hesitated even longer before answering. "Yes," he said finally, "I expect he is. It's been hard to live with Dad since times got so bad and he lost his job. But I can tell you one thing—Dad isn't nearly as bad as Josh thinks he is."

So, I thought, Joey too! Mom and Lonnie and now, Joey. All with a warm spot for Stefan Grondowski. Well and good. Let them keep their kind feelings for him; I didn't care. Maybe I'd starve in the years ahead, or maybe I'd get a job and be able to do the things I'd dreamed of doing. A lot of maybes, but among them there was one certainty: I would never go back and offer my hand in friendliness to Stefan Grondowski; never would I sit at his table again. Never! I found myself clutching big handfuls of grass as I lay there with the waves of anger running all through me.

But hope got the better of my rage as the big truck counted off the miles and the air grew warmer and the sky brighter with sunlight. We were driving into a new world, a kinder world where Lonnie would help me find a job, where things were going to be right with me for a change. I didn't intend to let thoughts of Dad spoil this new hope for me.

It wasn't long until we entered Louisiana and found ourselves on curving roads so unlike the straight highways of the Midwest. We drove past dozens of beautiful old plantation homes of a kind

85

that I had seen only in moving pictures. We were soon in the bayou country, dark with forests of pine and oak, of magnolia and cypress all draped with shaggy hangings of moss, gray and forlorn-looking. At a cafe where we stopped for lunch, we overheard some men speaking in a foreign tongue as they sat at the counter eating.

"That's mixed-up French," Lonnie told us. "Cajun talk. You'll hear a lot of it down in these parts."

I began to feel a little scared. This was a world of warmth and softness, good to feel after the harsh winter we had just left, but it was an alien world of strange trees and marshes, of unfamiliar language. I supposed the carnival would seem alien too, and I wondered how I would dare to ask for a job in a place so strange and, what was more than likely, so unfriendly to a stray kid asking for a job that a dozen local kids may have been wanting. I had heard over and over during the fall and early winter, "We've got kids here too, you know. We have to look after our own. We don't have enough for them and tramp-kids too." To ask for a job was almost like begging. I hated for Lonnie to see me rejected and humiliated when I begged for work.

Lonnie had to make several inquiries, but finally one evening we came upon it, the carnival we'd driven hundreds of miles to find. We found it lying before us in an open meadow only a few miles out of Baton Rouge. It was in full swing,

bright with hundreds of colored light bulbs, noisy
with the shouting of barkers and the laughter of
children and the blaring music of a merry-go-
round which dominated the center of the scene.
There was a Ferris wheel, too, with a few children
strapped in the seats, and on a circular track
there were a half dozen little cars with a great
cover of canvas falling in accordion folds over
them to give the effect of a giant caterpillar.
There were roulette wheels with cheap little
prizes attached—chewing gum, candy bars, occasionally a quarter or a half dollar. There were
tents where barkers urged us to have our for-
tunes told. We were invited to see a bearded lady,
a man with flippers instead of arms, a wild man
from the jungles of Borneo. We passed shooting
galleries and booths where the prizes for knock-
ing down a sand-filled dummy were plaster dolls
with enormous painted eyes or net stockings filled
with candy.

A clown on high stilts staggered toward us and
fell in front of Joey. People nearby laughed when
Joey tried politely to help the fallen figure and
the clown suddenly sprang to his feet and pretended to trounce Joey as if my brother had been
responsible for the fall.

We shuffled through the curled wood shavings
that covered the ground, inspecting and admiring
everything around us. The whole scene made me
remember when Dad had taken us to the amusement parks in Chicago long ago when I was little.

87

The memory made me feel very lonely for a minute, but I fought away any such loneliness with a stubborn resolve not to remember anything good about Dad.

After an hour or so we finally found a tent with the name *Pete Harris* painted on a placard above the opening. We went inside and found our man.

He was a short, rather fat man, neither friendly nor unfriendly. He and Lonnie talked quietly together for a time while Joey and I waited at a distance pretending to be interested in the people who passed by. Then Pete Harris called us over to his desk. He told us that the waitress who had given us his name was indeed his cousin. He seemed to like her; I got the impression that he wanted to help us as a favor to her.

It was plain, though, that he was worried. "I don't know," he said, rubbing the back of his neck with a big handkerchief. "To tell you the truth, I just don't know how long this show is goin' to hang together. Times ain't good for havin' fun. People ain't lettin' go of their money anymore; awful lot of people ain't got any money to let go of. I don't know whether I can afford to take on anybody more or not."

Lonnie was sympathetic. "I know. Company I haul for is laying off more drivers every week. May feel the axe myself, any time now. I know exactly how tight things are. Still, I wish you would at least hear the boy play. All of us in your cousin's cafe that night last week were kind of amazed at how he got music out of an old piano that was ready for the junk heap."

Pete Harris kept on mopping his neck and frowning at me. Then he glanced at Joey, and his face relaxed a little. "Hi ya, sport," he said, and he put his arm around Joey's shoulders in the way that most people reacted to my brother. Then he turned to me again. "All right, come on. Won't cost me anything to hear you play a little. Far as a job goes, though, I just don't know."

He led the way, and we followed him inside a tent where a piano was shoved in among chairs loaded with a lot of ruffly-looking dresses, a couple of chests with open boxes of powder and hairpins on top of them, and any number of battered suitcases and hatboxes. I glanced at Lonnie and saw that he was anxious. Pete Harris looked tired and skeptical. He motioned me to the piano as if he wanted to get the playing over and be rid of me quickly.

I played a few popular numbers, syncopating them with as much of a flair as I could. I tried to smile and look confident, patting my left foot lightly and swaying a little with the beat of my music. All the time I was thinking, "Give me a chance, Pete Harris; come on, give me a chance."

He drew his mouth down at the corners when I turned on the bench to face him. He looked at Lonnie rather than at me and nodded. "The kid's not bad," he said, reaching up to rub his head.

No Promises in the Wind

Lonnie sat astride a chair facing the back. He looked nonchalant. I might have felt that he was bored with the whole thing if I hadn't known better. "That's right," he said. "Josh handles that keyboard pretty well. I have an idea that a lot of people are going to like his music, not only because it's good, but because they like to see a kid doing this sort of thing. Not many kids his age play like that. . . ."

"If times were good, I'd take him in a minute," Harris said, "but they ain't good. Fact is, they're rotten." He looked at Joey again. "They've been rotten for you, too, haven't they, sport?"

"Yes, pretty rotten up until we met Lonnie." Joey was standing with both hands in his pockets, his thin face very sober. "But we can't expect Lonnie to take care of us any longer. We're not his kids."

Nobody said anything for a long time, and during that silence I felt as heavy as lead inside. Joey was right. We were not Lonnie's kids; we couldn't go on eating food that he paid for, promoting him to the job of being our dad when he hadn't asked for the honor. I had to face it: If there was no job for me at the carnival, Joey and I would have to start moving along on our own again. I wondered how begging would be around Baton Rouge.

Then to my amazement Pete Harris gave me a job. He had the look of a man who was doing a thing against his better judgment and finding it more than a little painful. He said, "I'm goin' to take you on, kid. You're pretty good. If you can learn to ballyhoo as well as you play, you just might be a good attraction." He paused and turned toward Joey. "I'll give your brother five dollars a week with grub and sleepin' space for the two of you. That okay with you boys?"

It was more than okay. It was wonderful, an offer to make the likes of us delirious. Our faces must have shown our joy, but Pete Harris didn't look joyful. He glanced at Lonnie, and I saw him shake his head slightly with a smile that looked grim rather than happy. Then he told us to come on outside and he'd show us where we could bunk for the night. He said he'd get me ready for work the next morning.

We followed him out to a tent on the edge of the meadow where there were dozens of cots lined up in long rows. "Men and boys sleep here," Harris told us. "A few have their families in box-cars out on the sidings—most don't have families at all—at least not here. I'll put you boys togeth-er down here at the end. The two dwarf men will be your neighbors. Edward C. is a fine little guy; Blegan is rattlebrained and gossipy as an old woman, but you don't need to pay any attention to him. They'll show you where the grub tent is in the morning. You come where you found me tonight, and I'll get you ready for work." He sighed as if he were tired and extended his hand to Lonnie. "Glad to have made your acquaintance.

No Promises in the Wind

I'll do right by the kids—long as I can. Like I told you, I just don't know...."

Lonnie had to leave us. He would drive most of the night to make up the time he'd lost in finding the carnival and Pete Harris for us. I was sorry for the delay and told him so, but he insisted that it didn't matter. "I wanted to see you with a job before I left you," he said as we walked back to the truck with him. "This is not exactly great, but it's a job. Maybe it will lead to something better— a guy can never tell."

We stood leaning against the big wheels of the truck. That truck had come to seem like home. I hated to give it up.

Lonnie handed me a scrap of paper with the name *Lon Bromer* written on it. I hadn't known his full name before. Underneath was a street address in Omaha, Nebraska. "This is where I live when I'm home," he told me. "I'll be back down here in a couple of weeks if I'm not laid off. If I make it back, I'll look you up. If not, let me hear how you're getting along."

"I'll do that, Lonnie; I sure will," I answered.

He stood looking at us as if he didn't quite know what to say. When he spoke, his voice didn't sound natural. "I'll have you two fellows on my mind. If you ever get into a real jam, you let me know. I'll be ready to help you best I can."

We shook hands, and he climbed up behind the wheel. As the truck moved away, he waved to us and Joey put into words what I secretly felt my-

92

No Promises in the Wind

self. He said, "If I was a little kid, I'd start bawlin' and run right after that truck."

I couldn't say much of anything. It didn't occur to me to tell Joey that he *was* still a little kid. Somehow I knew better.

We didn't feel any interest in the sights of the carnival after Lonnie left. It had been a long day, and the hard cots Pete Harris had assigned to us felt comfortable and good to our tired bodies. I lay awake for a long time trying to make myself realize that I was very lucky. Five dollars a week with food for Joey and me and a sheltered place to sleep meant a streak of luck that would have seemed impossible only a week before. It didn't matter that the carnival was a strange and bewildering place or that I was scared. It was nothing, I told myself, compared to the fear of cold and hunger which Joey and I had just experienced in Nebraska. That was true, certainly, but a fear of strange people was different. I couldn't explain it, but somehow I had felt more confidence alone with Joey as we scrounged for survival than I did that night in the midst of a crowd of people busy with the business of providing pleasure. "You don't make good sense," I told myself as sleep began to close in on me. I dreamed in what must have been the early hours of the night because I was aware of the monotonous music ground out by the merry-go-round, music that gradually receded and became the hum of big tires on a concrete road.

93

The dwarf men woke us the next morning. They were strange little people with old faces and bodies no larger than a five-year-old child's. One of them clambered up on Joey's bed and began to beat him with tiny wrinkled hands. The other, a much quieter and more dignified little man with a great hump on his back, stood at a distance and looked at us with grave interest.

"Get up if you want breakfast, you new guys," the noisy one squeaked at us. He wanted to know our names, where we were from, what our act was. His questions rattled out, one after the other, and yet I don't think he was really interested in any answers. He did, however, seize upon my statement that I played the piano.

"Oh, great," he yelled shrilly. "Pete Harris needs a piano player like we need another cut in wages. Pete Harris is a fool, a crazy old fool, and you are a crazy young fool. You'd better find another job. You won't be playin' a piano here very long—not with box office receipts slidin' off to nothing."

"Why can't you behave yourself, Blegan?" the second little man asked sharply. "Pete asked us to bring these boys to breakfast—he didn't say anything about giving them a lecture." He extended his hand to me. "My name is Edward C. Kensington. Don't pay any attention to Blegan; he'll be a pest for a while and then lose all interest in you. I've seen it happen before."

Blegan was, in fact, something of a pest, much

like a chattering, irresponsible monkey and apparently having little in common with Edward C. Kensington except for the matter of size. He pattered after Joey, plaguing him with insistent questions. "Why aren't you home with your mama, little sweet child?" he asked.

"I'm an orphan," Joey answered shortly, and he very pointedly ignored Blegan's further questions. When we were dressed, we walked with Edward C. Kensington to the breakfast tent while Blegan scampered ahead of us, turning occasionally to come back and ask a question which had been answered five minutes before.

At the tent there were fifty or more people seated on wooden benches at long, narrow tables. Here Blegan found his wife who had just arrived from the women's sleeping tent. They embraced lovingly and sat close together, eating from the same cereal bowl until an argument started and their shrill anger could be heard all through the tent. A few people laughed; others shrugged and paid no attention to them. We tried to ignore them, but when they upset the cereal bowl and splashed us with its contents, Edward C. Kensington led us to a place farther down the table near quieter neighbors.

"You'll find lots of pleasant people here in spite of the bad impression you're getting from those two," Edward C. Kensington told us. "We carnies are not a bad sort, really. Of course, the circus people rather look down their noses at us, but we

can't be bothered by that. Some of the finest
people I know are carnies—people like Emily.
You'll meet Emily soon; she's very dear to those
of us who appreciate quality." He sounded prim
and a little pompous, but we liked him. He asked
us to call him Edward C.

"The C stands for Courage," he said, smiling at
Joey. "Many times the pain in my hump has been
so bad, I've needed to remember that my middle
name is Courage." He turned to his breakfast
again, and his voice took on a brisker tone. "Well,
now, enough of that. Plenty of other people in
this world have their woes, too. Take that fellow
at the table opposite us—that is Ellsworth, the
man with flippers instead of arms. The man feeding him is Gorby, the sword swallower. They
travel together. Never say anything more than
'Good day' to any of us. Very reserved gentlemen.

"Then there is Madam Olympia, the obese
lady." Edward C. coughed delicately behind his
hand. "She has a rather remarkable appetite.
Never passes the platter to anyone; just empties
whatever is on it to her own plate and pushes the
empty platter aside. A little joke among us—not
kind, I'm afraid, but we grab at a chance to laugh
whenever we can."

He helped Joey to a serving of scrambled eggs
and grits from one of the platters that was being
passed down the length of our table. "We eat well
here," he said. "Pete Harris wants us to be well
fed. He makes Emily come here for breakfast

because he knows she starves herself at home so that her children can have enough. She isn't supposed to have meals here—people living outside the grounds are paid something extra so they can feed themselves. Emily gets the brunt of some snide remarks from a few of the others, but Pete sees that she has breakfast every morning whether other people like it or not. He looks after Emily. She's a very special person around here."

"Is Emily a performer?" I asked, not particularly interested, but aware that Edward C. was expecting me to carry on at least a part of the conversation.

He was greatly amused at the question. "Emily is the most popular performer in the carnival," he told us. "In fact, it's Emily who is holding this show together. She wasn't trained for this sort of life. She has just mapped out an act through her own ingenuity, and it's a good one. You"ll see. You'll meet her before long."

I didn't say anything. I felt nervous and scared inside, and wished that Edward C. would not feel it necessary to tell us about any other people at the table. I would have liked for him just to be quiet a while.

He wasn't, though. He wanted to tell us that one of the men at the end of the table was a former bank teller and was now in charge of a shooting gallery, happy to get the job when the banks closed. A young-looking woman beside him had been a high school teacher, but had lost her job when it had been discovered that she was married. One job to a family had been the rule for school teachers, so now she was operating a roulette wheel. Edward C. didn't know what her husband was doing, probably nothing, since he had been a car salesman when times were such that cars could be sold. The wild man from Borneo who was carrying on what appeared to be a civilized conversation with his neighbor was, according to Edward C., a Cajun from the bayou country who had never been out of the state of Louisiana.

"We're a motley crew, we carnies," Edward C. said, and then interrupted himself with a happy shout. "There she is—there's Emily." He jumped up on the bench and waved toward the opening of the tent. "Here we are—over here, Emily."

She was a tall woman wearing a clown's costume of bright colors with a wide white ruff around her neck. Her shoes were great, flapping triangles of red leather, the toes extending a foot or more beyond the edge of her balloonlike trousers.

She came straight to the place where we sat and shook hands, first with Joey and then with me. "Pete asked me to find you and say 'hello.' I knew, though, that you were in good hands as long as you were with Edward C."

She seemed to me to be the most beautiful woman I had ever seen. I couldn't have described her at first; her hair, her eyes and mouth and smooth white skin, all combined to give an impression of beauty just as color and light and shadow and texture combine to make a picture beautiful long before the details are apparent. After a minute, I became conscious that her short hair was neither red nor gold, but a blend of both, that it lay in shining half-rings close to her head. I realized that her forehead was very wide and smooth, that her eyes were almost purple and shaded by long, thick lashes.

I must have stared at her too long. There was a quiet chuckle from Edward C. "Why are you so surprised, Josh? Haven't you ever seen a beautiful clown before?"

Joey was not so dazzled as I was; he had light words for Emily. "I didn't know ladies were ever clowns," he said, smiling. "I wouldn't think they'd like to make themselves ugly."

"They don't, Joey," Emily answered. "But they like to eat occasionally. And to see that their children eat. So when they get a chance to make some money at the business of clowning, they forget that they'd rather look pretty." She buttered a piece of toast and bit into it hungrily. "You must get acquainted with my boys," she said, again addressing Joey. "The oldest is about your age. The other two are eight and five. Sometimes they forget that I'm their mother. When they see me on the grounds, they call me Bongo, just as the other kids do."

"Should I call you Bongo?" Joey asked.

"It would be better. You see, no one outside the gates knows that I am a woman. Carnival and circus crowds think of all clowns as men. They might not like a clown named Emily."

Her voice was beautiful, and I loved beautiful voices in women. It had the quality of a little bell, I thought, and I longed to get at the piano to see if I could find the notes that would let me express Emily's voice in music. I was afraid that I couldn't, but I wanted to try.

Edward C. was speaking to Joey. "Emily's the greatest attraction of the carnival, Joey. People bring their children back night after night because of Bongo—"

"And the caterpillar," Emily interposed, "and the merry-go-round. We three—I don't know which of us rates top billing." She turned to me again. "You'll be playing and ballyhooing outside the girlie-show, Josh. Those ladies at the table off to the left are the dancers. It's a gyp-show—you'd just as well know it. People pay a dime and expect to see either some pretty girls or some beautiful dancing, and they see women who are no longer pretty and dancing that is only third-rate. It's a gyp—Pete will admit it, and a lot of people will complain to you about it. But the dancers have to eat, too, you know. They're not very good, but then I'm not the funniest clown in the world either. There isn't a performance on the grounds that is really top-notch. But Pete keeps us, and

100

we limp along. At least we have a little food each
day. A lot of people would envy us for that."

I nodded. "I know all about being hungry—and
grateful for a job," I said.

She put her hand on mine, and her eyes were
full of kindness. "I know, Josh. Pete has told me
what he learned about you from the truck driver.
Pete wants very much to help you and Joey."

"He seems like a very kind gentleman," I said.
But I wasn't thinking of Pete Harris as I spoke. I
was looking at the oval of her face and the gentle
concern in her eyes. There was a kindness and a
sweetness about her that made me forget everything in the world except the fact that she was
there beside me. The thought came to me suddenly and clearly: This is what it means to be in love.
I love someone who is kind and beautiful. I love
someone who is a clown.

She was talking about Pete Harris when I became conscious of her words again. "He is a good
man," she was saying quietly. "He has his weaknesses, but he's good. You can count on Pete if
you play fair." She turned and smiled at the
dwarf man. "Isn't that so, Edward C?"

He puckered his mouth until it was like a tiny
rosette in the middle of his face. "You and I know
it is so, Emily. The boys will realize it, too, when
they're better acquainted with him."

Emily said nothing more. She picked up her
fork and began to eat the food Edward C. passed
to her. She did not look up until the dancers came

by. One of them spoke to her; the others didn't look in her direction. A woman with bleached, harsh-looking hair looked at me and smiled. She said, "Hi, there, big fellow." Another woman gave the speaker a disgusted look. "Don't tip the cradle, Florrie. Let Pete Harris and his clown take care of the kid."

Emily's face didn't change expression. She said, "You'll find all kinds of people here, Josh. You'll have to play by ear for a while. You'll have to be very careful."

When she noticed that Edward C. and Joey and I had finished our meal, she asked us to wait until she'd finished eating. "Pete wants me to trim your hair before you start on your job," she said. "I'm kind of an expert at barbering. There are three redheads at home who have to be trimmed every so often. I'm getting pretty good at the job."

So we waited, and then with Edward C. striding beside me and Emily walking hand in hand with Joey, we went into one of the tents where she draped a towel over my shoulders and worked on my hair with quick sure snips of her scissors. She trimmed Joey too while she was at it, and then leaned back in a chair and regarded us with satisfaction. "You both have well-shaped heads— that's very important for men. More important in my mind than height or width of shoulder." She put her hands up to her own short hair and pulled it vigorously as if she were trying to lessen a tightness of her scalp. "You can go to Pete now. He'll tell you what you're to do today. I'm going to rest here a bit before I put on my makeup."

"You're tired, Emily. Your eyes show it," Edward C. said gently.

"I'm always tired, Edward C. I won't know how to behave if I ever find myself rested again." She smiled and gave us a little wave as if she were anxious that we get going.

"Emily is overworked," Edward C. told us as we walked along. "It's too much. A clown act is exhausting in itself. Besides that she has the boys to care for and the anxiety about all the tomorrows ahead of her." He shook his head. "I worry about Emily. I'm so fond of her."

It was a bright, warm morning, the third of December, and as beautiful as if it had been the third of May back home. There was a general bustling about as workers prepared for the opening of the gates at eleven o'clock. People in charge of concessions were getting their equipment set up; kegs of lemonade, cartons of cotton candy and pink taffy, loads of dolls and toys, were being set out in the various booths. Men were inspecting the machinery that kept the merry-go-round and the Ferris wheel operating, and performers were going around with costumes folded over their arms. Some of them were sitting in front of a tent with needle and thread, repairing damages made to their clothing the night before.

Joey and I seemed to be the only ones who didn't know our way around.

We found Pete Harris busy at bookwork in his tent. He looked up and nodded as the three of us entered. "Morning, Edward C. Glad you're taking care of the boys." He looked at me approvingly. "I see Emily has worked on your hair a little. Looks better. Looks a lot better. Trust Emily. She can do anything, that girl, anything. Wish I could pay her what she's worth. Can't, though. Times are rotten. Guess I told you that yesterday, didn't I, sport? As if you didn't know."

He gave me a pair of tight-fitting pants, a bright red and yellow shirt, and a checkered vest with wide fringe dangling at the bottom. I looked like a fool in the outfit, but Pete said the loud colors would help to get attention.

After I was decked out, we went over to the tent where I had played the night before. The piano had been moved onto a small platform outside the tent, and my job was to play popular songs as loudly and flashily as possible while I called out to anyone approaching, urging them to go inside to see the dancers. I must say that they were the prettiest girls in the country, that they were wearing the shortest skirts and doing the most daring dances outside the dance halls of Paris. I was supposed to sway and bounce all over the piano bench as if I were having all the fun in the world; I was to grin and wink and urge people to pay their dimes and step inside.

No Promises in the Wind

It was a painful thing for me to do. I had always been shy and reserved. That was one reason I hadn't had many friends at Penn High. Howie had been able to clown when he accompanied my piano at school dances, but even with the kids my own age, I hadn't been able to do more than allow the expression on my face to show how much I enjoyed playing.

Now I would have to play the silly fool for hour after hour; my antics were just as important, Pete Harris said, as the loudness and gaiety of the music. I didn't like it; this silly, false routine was not what I had hoped for. But that didn't matter. It was a job. It meant five beautiful dollars a week. I didn't for one second think of refusing it, but as I took my place at the piano, I made Edward C. take Joey away. I wouldn't have him watching. And I hoped fervently that Emily would not come near. That was one thing I didn't believe I could take.

Chapter Six

Emily was, indeed, the star attraction of the carnival. People who couldn't afford to spend money at the sideshows would still bring their children back night after night to laugh at the antics of the clown they called Bongo. They never heard the clown speak; words didn't matter. The fun lay in seeing the tall figure sprawl at the slightest impact with a tree, a chair, another person; of seeing the dull-witted bewilderment with which the clown got out of one troubled situation into another. The Blegans and Edward C. scampered around Bongo, teasing and tormenting, luring him into trouble and then pretending to pummel and pinch him to punish his stupidity. The kids loved it, because, as Emily explained to me, they saw

Edward C. and the Blegans as being little like themselves, and seeing a grown-up clown outwitted by the childish-looking dwarf men was not only funny but satisfying to the young.

Personally I could have clouted the little monsters, and I told Emily so, but she only smiled and asked me to think of the clowns I had once laughed at and to remember what it was that made me laugh. She was right. I had been a little monster too; I had been gleeful when the silly clown fell flat or was punished for being stupid. But that was long before I knew a clown named Emily.

Each day's work was long and strenuous for her. She was on the grounds constantly, mingling with the crowds, bumping and tumbling in a continuous effort to win a few laughs from people who were not too ready for laughter. At closing time she would gather her three sleeping children from Pete Harris's tent and would walk wearily outside the gates and over to the boxcar which was their home. She nearly always stopped beside my piano to say good-night; I would wait for her there if my chores were finished first. Emily's good-night came to be a small spot of joy for me in a day that was often tedious and monotonous.

She always ate breakfast with us before she put her makeup on for the day. After that I seldom saw her except at a distance during working hours, but there were a few times when the crowds were nearly gone and the lights dimmed that Emily had a chance to stand beside my piano and listen as I played the way I wanted to play. Then I would improvise some of the melodies that were in my mind, trying out variations in minor keys, softly and with a tenderness that was all for her. Eventually I'd return to the original major key with a lot of fanfare which was my way of boasting to her of my skill. Mostly she would just stand and listen, smiling to herself, but saying nothing. One night, though, she leaned forward and spoke to me softly. "You have a gift, Josh; don't let these times make you lose sight of it."

I was restless during these weeks. Joey and I kept waiting for Lonnie to return, and when he didn't, we knew that he must have lost his job as he had feared. I took three dollars out of the precious ten that Pete Harris had given me after my first two weeks of work and put them in a letter to Lonnie. Joey added a dollar of the money he had earned at running errands, and we wrote Lonnie that this was the first installment on the money we owed him. We felt good when we mailed that letter.

We bought one another gifts for Christmas and were so excited about buying something other than food that we opened our packages days before Christmas arrived. I bought a bright blue shirt for Joey with a chocolate bar slid in the breast pocket. And he gave me an imitation leather wallet to hold my newly acquired wealth. I don't know when a gift had ever pleased me so much. That wallet gave me a sense of well-being when I put it into my hip pocket; moreover, it had several interesting compartments as well as an identification card which I filled out proudly. There was a line which stated, "In case of accident, please notify——————." I started to write "Stefan Grondowski" on that line; then I thought better of it and wrote "Lon Bromer" and added the Omaha address he'd given us.

Still, in spite of the unforgiving streak in me, I kept thinking of home as Christmas drew near. On the warm, gentle nights when the noise of the carnival had subsided, I would often take long walks, wondering as I walked if there were still the lines of men in front of employment offices back in Chicago, wondering if Kitty had managed to get a job, wondering a hundred things about Mom. When Joey wrote a note home to tell them of my job, to let them know we were well, I gave him a dollar to add to the one he was placing in the letter. Joey wrote, "Josh and I are sending you this money for Christmas." He asked me if I wanted to sign the letter, and for a moment I really wanted to write my name beside his. But I said, "No, I guess not," and he sealed the letter without saying anything more about it.

I thought a great deal about Emily during these days, not the Emily who clowned all day, but the Emily who met us at breakfast and stopped beside my piano late at night—the beautiful Emily with great purple eyes and a sweet oval face above the clown's ruff.

They were sad, these thoughts of Emily. Somewhere I had gained the impression that love makes one happy, but that was not true for me. Love only hurt me; it hurt the way uncertainty and hopelessness did.

One night as I waited for her to come past my piano and say good-night, I heard her youngest boy wailing sleepily as she herded the three of them home. When I saw her stoop to lift the boy in her arms, I ran to her and offered to carry him piggy-back to the boxcar. He whimpered at first and then let his head droop to my neck where he sighed and went back to sleep. Emily walked beside me, hand in hand with the other two boys, and none of us spoke as we picked our way along the railroad ties that led up to their home.

When we laid the children on their beds, I stepped outside and Emily followed me. She sat down on the lowest step of the car, pulling the skullcap from her bright hair.

"Sit down for a minute, Josh," she said. "I've been wanting to talk to you." She paused, looking at me directly. "Is something troubling you lately?"

"No," I said. "Just the blues."

"It's a time for the blues, isn't it?"

"I ought to be thankful that I have a job. Well, I am. It's just . . ." I didn't know how to finish the sentence.

"You're lonely, Josh; I've realized that. It's too bad that there aren't any young people of your age in the carnival. I've been wishing I knew some nice girl, someone you'd enjoy taking to a movie now and then."

I shook my head. We both sat silent and stared out into the night for a while. Then before I knew what I was going to say, I blurted out what was pent up inside me. "I wish you were a girl, Emily. I'd give anything in the world if you were a girl my age." As soon as the words were out, I grew rigid with dismay at what I had revealed.

She looked down at the long flapping shoes of her clown costume for a few moments; then she turned to me and smiled.

"If I were a girl your age, I'd be very proud to know you cared for me, Josh."

"But you don't like it that I—that I care for you now, do you?"

She leaned forward and clasped her hands around her knees. Her face was very sober, and there was a slight frown between her eyes.

"You know, Josh, there are women who become very vain when a younger man tells them what you've told me. I'm not vain—I think I'm grateful. It's right to be grateful for every bit of honest affection that comes one's way, isn't it?"

"I was afraid you'd think I was a fool," I muttered.

"Then you don't know me very well. I think of

111

you as a sensitive, talented boy—a bit on the stubborn side, but never a fool."

She leaned toward me. I think she started to kiss my cheek, but she changed her mind and offered me her hand instead. Then she laid her left hand over mine and made the handshake a little caress.

I didn't want to leave her, but I knew I must. When I got to my feet, I stood looking down at her for a minute, and she smiled at me. It was a smile, I realized, such as she so often gave to Joey.

"Good-night, dear Josh," she said. "Good-night and thank you."

The next morning at breakfast Emily turned to Edward C. "I think we must all drag ourselves out of the blues for Christmas, Edward C. The carnival will be closed Christmas Eve so why don't you and the boys come over to my place for cocoa and molasses cookies. Would you like that?"

I suppose our faces showed our delight. "It's an honor, Josh," Edward C. told me later. "Emily keeps so much to herself. I can't remember a time when she has invited any of us to her home. It's obvious that you and Joey and I are special to her."

We began immediately to think of a gift which we might take to her on Christmas Eve. Joey thought a box of candy would be right; I wanted to buy something more feminine, more personal. There were pretty bottles of perfume at one of the concessions. I very much wanted to buy perfume for Emily.

But Edward C. was sternly practical. "She needs money so much, Josh, with that family of growing boys. I think we should find a bright box and fill it with dimes, ten dimes from each of us. Joey can polish them till they're shiny, and we'll get one of the ladies to tie a ribbon around the box for us. Emily will appreciate it, boys; believe me, I know she'll appreciate it at this time more than she would either candy or perfume."

And so we followed his advice, and the small box of silver did look like a very nice gift. It was not what I really wanted to give Emily, but I had to admit that Edward C. was probably wise in his suggestion. Emily would have very little occasion to wear perfume. I hoped, though, that a day might come when I could buy her something lovely, something right for a beautiful woman.

The three of us, well scrubbed and brushed, went over to Emily's boxcar home early the evening before Christmas. She met us at the door, and for the first time I saw her dressed like a woman with no hint of the clown about her. She wore a cotton dress, the colors of which were faded, probably from many washings, but a lovely dress for all that, with a full skirt that swayed gracefully when she walked. But it was her earrings that made Emily look like a queen—large, bright hoops that were much the same red-gold color as her hair. They swung against her cheeks, catching the light and looking very gay and splendid.

Edward C. and Joey found words more easily than I did. They told her how beautiful she looked, how nice it was to see her in a dress instead of a clown's costume, how beautiful her earrings were. She smiled and stooped to kiss each of them on the forehead; then she looked at me as if she were waiting for what I had to say. "You look very nice, Emily," I told her, and she said, "Thank you, Josh," and kissed me too.

Then suddenly the evening was no longer wonderful for me. We stepped inside, and there at the table with her youngest boy on his lap and the other two beside him sat Pete Harris, short and fat and glistening a little, but looking relaxed and pleased.

"Hello—hello, gentlemen," he called out in his raspy voice. "How are you, Edward C? Brought your boys with you, eh? Just look at young sport here. You're gettin' fat, boy; you're gettin' some meat on you." He poked Joey in the stomach and then held out his hand to me. "How're you doin', Paderewski?" he asked.

Emily stood beside his chair smiling and looking happy. "Pete surprised us with roast chickens and pralines; now we can have a *real* Christmas party, Joey. The boys could hardly wait until you got here."

Joey was beaming. He handed her the box of

dimes. "This is for you, Emily, from Edward C. and Josh and me," he said.

Emily opened the package, her eyes shining at first and then filling with tears. She held the box of dimes over for Pete Harris to see. He nodded approvingly. "That's a real fine present, boys," he said. Then he looked up at Emily. "You couldn't ask for a nicer one, could you, hon?"

He called her "hon". He spoke to my beautiful Emily as if she belonged to him, and in the next moment she was saying that the dimes from us and the earrings from Pete were making this the happiest Christmas she had known in a long time.

And so Pete Harris had given her the earrings that made her look like a queen, and I, who wanted to give her something lovely and feminine, had been persuaded to share in a gift of dimes that would probably be used to buy grits and oatmeal for her boys.

I think Edward C. saw the look of disappointment on my face, for he hurried to make an explanation to Emily. "You know, my dear, Josh wanted to buy you perfume. And you're so lovely tonight that I'm sorry I dissuaded him. You should have had gifts that were more personal— gifts that would have allowed us to tell you how pretty you are."

She put her arm around the little man's shoulders, but she looked at me when she spoke. "No, Edward C., you three couldn't have given me a finer gift than the box of dimes. And every time I

115

use some of them for food or medicine, I'll say, 'This is my gift of white gloves from Joey; this is a lace handkerchief from Edward C.—and this is another drop of French perfume from our musician, from Josh!' "

Her words helped a little. Not much, but a little. It would have been better if Pete Harris had kept quiet. But he didn't. He said, "You were on the right track, Edward C. Emily needs those dimes. This ain't a year for lace handkerchiefs and perfume. Right, hon?"

But it was a year for earrings from Pete Harris.

It was a long, unhappy evening. There was food and laughter. There was a moment when Pete Harris disappeared, and returned a few minutes later wearing a mask and white beard, bringing small toys to Emily's children and a last-minute gift for Joey—a pocketknife, obviously an old one with Pete Harris's initials carved in the bone handle, but a gift which nonetheless brought considerable joy to Joey. Later all of us went across to the carnival grounds and gathered around my piano. While I played the old carols, the others sang, and the music under the quiet sky was beautiful. Emily and her boys with Edward C. sang some of the carols in the Cajun tongue, and they sounded sweet and strange, a little mysterious. It should have been a beautiful evening, but it wasn't for me. I was glad when I could get away and be alone.

In the days that followed, I was edgy and unhappy. Joey noticed it and stayed away from me most of the time, spending many hours by himself practicing on Howie's banjo. One day on the grounds a small group of people gathered around him as he sang and accompanied himself on the banjo. They liked the picture, I think, of the slender boy singing and strumming out a simple run of chords; they liked it so much that Harris allowed Joey to roam around the carnival grounds with his banjo. He picked up a little store of nickels and dimes in that way, but he didn't talk to me about it. I had been sharp with him on too many occasions lately. He left me to myself.

I felt angry with everyone those days, with Joey for no reason, with Edward C. because I had an idea that he understood too well the secret I tried to guard, with Pete Harris for presuming to love Emily. Most of all I was angry with Emily. She had been tender and kind, and then she had betrayed me by allowing an old man to call her endearing names, to give her the kind of gift I wanted to give her. I felt ashamed of my feelings, but they were beyond the control of reason.

The dancer named Florrie, who told me that her name was actually Florinda, took to stopping at my piano oftener when nobody else was around. She was not attractive; her eyes were watery-looking, and her mouth was loose and gave her a vacant, stupid look. Sometimes she seemed to like me, although she was angry when

I addressed her as "Ma'am," but whether she liked me or not was of no consequence to me. My only reason for a mild friendliness toward her was that both Edward C. and Pete Harris warned me against her. Something negative in me made me pretend to like her better than I did.

Florinda teased me about my sober appearance. "Don't you ever smile about nothin', big fellow?" she asked one night. "Was there some law up north that kept big fellows like you from ever gettin' a smile on their mouths?"

"There's nothing much to smile about, Florinda," I answered.

"You come out with me some night after workin' hours and I'll take you places where there's plenty of smiles. You got money in your pocket now. You can afford to treat yourself and me to some nice smile places."

"I have to save my money," I answered shortly. "I've been hungry because I didn't have money. I don't believe in spending it in smile places."

Florinda moved her shoulders in a gesture that repelled me. "I know what's eatin' you, big fellow. It's the clown. I've seen you lookin' calf-eyed at her. Well, listen, kid—she's Pete Harris's woman. Don't get no big ideas. That clown belongs to Pete. So you just better be a good boy and keep your eyes off her."

I was icy toward Florinda after that, but she had her revenge for her words haunted me. "She's Pete Harris's woman. That clown belongs
118

to Pete." They were the words of a cheap, venomous woman, I knew, but I remembered the earrings. I remembered that Pete Harris had called Emily "hon."

For many nights I no longer waited for Emily to come past and say good-night. Deliberately I left my post early sometimes, and though I paid for my rebuff to Emily with hours of sleeplessness and regret, the stubborn Grondowski part of me would settle for no other behavior. At breakfast when Emily joined us, I was far on the other side of Joey and Edward C., so far away that I could only nod to her. I even talked to the Blegans in order to seem too preoccupied for a morning conversation with her. And the Blegans repaid me with more gossip: Had I heard that Pete Harris was soon to marry his clown? Oh, what a fool Pete Harris was to take on three redheaded brats for the privilege of marrying a redheaded clown! This from the Blegans.

One night I waited for her. She was alone, the children having been put to bed earlier by Edward C. She came up to the piano as she had in the weeks before Christmas. "Good-night, Josh," she said quietly and started to walk on without saying anything more.

I jumped up from the piano bench and went to her side. "May I walk home with you?" I asked.

She was very grave. "Yes, of course," she answered. "I haven't talked with you for a long time."

When we reached her doorsteps, she sat down and faced me. "Well, Josh?" she said finally.

"How can you do it, Emily?" I asked desperately.

"Do what?" she asked.

"You know very well. How can you marry Pete Harris? How can you do a thing like that?"

She was silent for a long time. Then she reached over and took my hand. I felt myself go weak while my hand rested in hers.

"Josh, once many years ago I loved someone who didn't even know that I existed. I loved him so much—and I hated the girl he loved, a girl older and more sophisticated than I was. I suffered in those awful weeks before they were married, but the days and months smoothed things out for me. To tell you the truth, I have almost forgotten what he was like or why I loved him. But I know my love was sharp and hurtful while it lasted. I feel sorry for the little Emily I was then and for the agony she went through."

"Yes. What are you trying to tell me?"

"I don't know." She drew a long breath. "I'm not sure what I want to tell you. I'm just saying what's in my mind at the moment."

"This is in my mind, Emily. People are saying that you're Pete Harris's woman. Is that right?"

"There's a hate-quality about that statement that makes me suspect it came from Florinda or the Blegans—or both." She took her hands away from mine and clasped them in her lap. "No, I am not Pete Harris's 'woman' in the sense they say it. But I am going to marry Pete. And you must listen to me, Josh. I have to tell you a few things."

She looked out into the night as she spoke, and at first her voice sounded colder than I'd ever heard it, but after a minute it warmed and she was Emily again.

"Pete is a good man. He's not handsome or well-educated or polished. He's not rich—he's never likely to be rich because he cares too much for everyone who has too little. Pete's not what is called a catch, but he's loyal and kind and decent. He knew my husband and me here in Baton Rouge several years ago; when Carl was dying, Pete was like an older brother to him; when my boys and I were left terribly poor, he created a job for me here in the carnival, a job for which I had no training. He has looked after us and protected us—isn't that enough? Does he need any higher credentials?"

"But he's an old man," I said bitterly. "He's too old for you."

"Pete's forty-five, Josh. That's fifteen years older than I am. And I'm that much older than you are. Fifteen years doesn't matter awfully when you care for one another, does it?"

I didn't even answer for a long time. Finally I muttered, "All right. Just forget you ever knew me. We'll be strangers from now on."

She didn't move as I got up to walk away, but

she spoke, and although her voice was very low, I heard every word. She said, "There are so many things that make life hurtful these days, Josh. If we're to be strangers, that is just one more painful thing. But if that's it, I'll have to accept it. I hope you'll change your mind."

I left without answering her, and I lay awake for most of the night, miserable at having hurt her, but the memory of her defense of Pete Harris was a bitterness as great as my misery.

The next morning as we walked to breakfast, I noticed that Edward C. was looking at me with unusual kindness. Edward C. was a wise little man; I was sure he knew much more about me than I had ever told him. When I mentioned that I was going to take a place at another table because I wanted to speak to the former bank teller about something, Edward C. nodded and made no comment. As a matter of fact, I hardly knew the former bank teller, and after we had exchanged nods, we ate our breakfast in complete silence. I didn't look across the room to the place where Joey and Edward C. welcomed Emily.

Joey waited for me after the two others had walked on toward the dressing-room tents. "You hurt Emily's feelings this morning, Josh," he told me. "And Edward C.'s too. I don't know how you can do a thing like that."

"You mind your business, Joey; I'll take care of mine," I answered. I didn't want to say that, but the words were out, and there was no recalling them. Joey didn't reply, but he looked me directly in the eye, and the expression on his face was not that of the adoring little brother. There was a cold, critical look in his eyes; I had a feeling that if I had wanted to fight, Joey would have fought right back.

The weather that day was chillier than it had been since we reached Louisiana. The radio told about blizzards and sub-zero temperatures back home and all through the northern part of the nation. Fringes of that cold had apparently moved down to us, and the people, unaccustomed to chill winds, were miserable. Dozens of children were scuttling along the railroad tracks to pick up bits of coal and wood for fires in the boxcar homes. In the carnival tents, lights were left burning to provide a little warmth.

The carnival crowd had dwindled to almost nothing during the day. The dancers didn't even bother to put on their act in the evening after a whole day of facing empty chairs in front of their pavilion.

Freed of my duties for the night, I wandered beyond the meadow where the carnival lay, walking on and on with the hope that I'd get so tired I could go right to sleep when I returned to our tent. But long after weariness had worked down to bone depth, I sat leaning against a tall pine by the side of the road, facing my loneliness. I should have been used to the feeling; it had been with me for many weeks but never quite so heavy as it was that night. I sat there remembering Mom and Kitty, remembering Howie and Miss Crowne. I wanted to see Lonnie again; I wanted so much to talk to him, and amazingly enough for a brief flash I wanted the dad I had once known. Most of all, I wanted someone near me who was tender and sweet, someone who was Emily, but a fifteen-year-old Emily who would wear the earrings I would give her and would sit close beside me while I played music that would tell her of my love.

The wind made a little sighing sound in the branches above me. I hated the wind. A bright morning, a moonlit night, a sunset sky—these might fill me with hope for happier times. Not the wind. It either lashed or cried or whispered little mysteries known only to itself. The wind never gave me hope; it never made any promises. I buried my head in my arms for a while.

It was late when I started back toward the carnival grounds. There was a glow in the sky above the grounds, the glow of the carnival lights I thought at first, but then I realized that the light did not flash and sparkle in a pattern of colors. It was like a purplish red cloud hovering over the grounds. It looked ominous.

I felt troubled and began to run; then I heard the noises of sirens and trucks. I smelled the bitter smell of burning canvas and leather, celluloid and oil.

'The carnival was in wild confusion when I got there. Fire trucks, police cars, and an ambulance were on the grounds, and everywhere there were people with drawn, white faces, their eyes reddened by smoke and tears. Half the tents were charred or in ashes. The merry-go-round stood silent in the midst of ruin, some of its gaily painted horses blackened with smoke. The cars that made up the giant caterpillar which so many children had loved were collapsed and smoldering. My piano was a distorted shell, and the dancers' pavilion was gone.

I found Joey with Emily and her boys and Edward C. They stood together outside Emily's boxcar, silent and almost unmoving, or so it seemed to me. The children showed signs of crying; the faces of Emily and Edward C. were full of despair.

They told me what had happened. An oil heater had been left burning in one of the tents. Something caught fire, no one knew how; but the wind had blown fragments of burning canvas from one tent to another, from one set of flimsy toys to a dressing tent where frills and ruffles flamed as readily as a box of matches. Joey had saved the banjo and our few belongings when he saw the fire spreading, but the tent where we had slept was a mass of red coals on the ground.

"Pete was planning to move the carnival farther south in a few weeks," Emily said. "Now, there's little left to move. I don't know whether

125

he can build another show or not—I can't bear to
ask him."

Florinda walked up to the steps where we were
standing. Her face was swollen with crying, and
she stepped stiffly, like a person walking in his
sleep. Her voice was shrill when she spoke to us.

"What's going to become of us? Answer me,
Emily. Answer me, Edward C. What's going to
happen to us? What are we going to do now?"

"We'll do whatever we can, Florinda," Emily
answered. "Maybe we'll scrub floors; there are
still people left who can afford to pay for having
their floors scrubbed. Maybe we'll scrub clothes
over a washboard. We'll do whatever we have
to do."

"But I'm a dancer," Florinda almost screamed.
No one said anything, and that apparently frightened and enraged her. "All right, I know what
you're thinking—you're thinking that I've passed
my best years. You're thinking that my legs are
lumpy and that nobody'll hire me—that I'm too
old to get another job. Well, maybe that's true.
This punk"—she turned on me—"this kid calling
me 'Ma'am'—trying to make me feel a hundred—
all right, punk, so I'm getting old and so I don't
have Pete Harris to look after me the way your
clown does—" She stopped in the middle of her
tirade and commenced to cry. "I've never done a
thing in my life except dance in the carnivals.
And now my legs are lumpy, and I'm getting too
old for the job. What am I going to do?"

No Promises in the Wind

Emily closed her eyes for a second and pressed her hands against her temples. Then she knelt on the step and drew Florinda down beside her. The rest of us walked a little distance away.

Florinda left after a half hour or so, and Emily went inside the car where she made cocoa for the children and coffee for the rest of us. Her face was different. It was ashy white and set in stern, hard lines. She didn't smile as she handed our cups to us.

The terror of the fire, the hysteria of Florinda, the fear and anxiety that had struck all of us, had made a stranger of Emily. She sat drinking her coffee and staring at the ruin before us. Edward C. put his small hand on hers once to remind her, I guess, of his presence and affection. She nodded in acknowledgment of his gesture, but that was all.

Then as we all sat together, grim and unhappy, Pete Harris came striding down the tracks and ran up the steps of the car. The room was dimly lighted, and I didn't recognize him at first, but Emily did. She ran to him and hid her face against his shoulder; he put his arms around her and held her close to him. I heard her say, "It's going to be all right, hon. We'll make it back. I promise you, we'll make it back. As long as I have you and the boys, I'm not scared about a comeback. . . ."

I watched them, and they were like two people far removed from me. Pete Harris was kind, he was gentle with Emily, and that was right. And

127

Emily—I knew, finally, that she could never have been the fifteen-year-old Emily I had dreamed about. Never. She was a woman nearer my mother's age than mine. But she had been kind. When I'd needed understanding most, Emily had been understanding. That was the way I would remember her—except once in a while, perhaps, when I'd see a beautiful woman wearing earrings of a certain red-gold color. And then, I knew, I'd remember a time when love was new and bewildering—and bitterly sweet.

Chapter Seven

Pete Harris said, "At least it's warm down here. I remember those Nebraska winters—they're killers. If it comes to begging again, better to be where you're warm even if you're hungry."

"Yes," I said, "I know you're right. Still . . ."

"You want to get back to that truck driver, don't you? He's kind of a daddy to you and Joey—ain't that so?"

I knew it was so, but I didn't like to admit it. I just bit my lip and said nothing.

"I'd like to help you, Josh, you know that. And after a few months I may be able to get a show of sorts on the road again. I'm not sure. Money's tight, but I think I'll be able to get something together. Right now, though, I'm about down to rock bottom, and I have to look out for Emily and the boys, you know. I wish I could help you till we're over the hump, because when I do get things movin' again, I'd like to have you in a better spot. But for the next six months or so— well, I just don't have the means to carry you over that long."

"I know you don't," I answered. "And I want you to know that I appreciate all you've done for me so far. As for Joey and me—you don't need to worry; we can get along. I've saved most of my money, and so has he. I've got eighteen dollars in my wallet."

"Yes? Well, that will take you pretty far if you're careful. You can hitchhike a lot, and you know how to live cheap. Maybe it's best you get back to that man in Nebraska. He liked you boys— I could see that. Whether he's able to help you or not is another matter. But to be near someone you like and trust, that's something to think about." He took out his wallet and removed two dollars. "I'll make that eighteen an even twenty, Josh. It's the best I can do. No, don't thank me; you've earned it. You made a lot of people stand around and listen to that piano. It was good for business—good as anything is these days. Well"— he held out his hand—"God bless you, kid; take care of the little sport."

We shook hands. I drew a long breath. I could accept Pete Harris now. I could accept many things—the different picture of Emily, the dishev-
130

eled little dream that had taken such a beating. Fine, I could accept everything. But I had to get away from them—so far away that I would never again hear Pete Harris call Emily "hon." I had to leave these soft skies that had given us so much comfort, had to get away from these people, kind as they had been to Joey and me. I knew it was a foolish thing to do. I wouldn't have dared to explain it, but I had to leave.

I went over to tell Emily good-bye that afternoon. She still looked white, and her voice didn't sound quite natural. The worry that gripped all of us had hit Emily hard, but there was no whining from her, no hysterics of the Florinda variety. She had a bag of molasses cookies packed for Joey and me, and one of pecans which her little boys wanted us to have. She searched around in her stored bedding until she found a wool blanket which she insisted that I take.

When I was ready to go, she held out her hand to me and as she had done that first night, gave the handshake added warmth by placing her left hand over mine.

"I'll always remember you, Josh, and I'll always be wishing the best for you. Will you write to me?"

"Yes," I answered, wondering what I would ever be able to say to her.

She handed me a piece of paper. "Send any letter to Pete at this Baton Rouge address. He'll see that I get it."

"Yes," I said again. I sounded like a stupid parrot, and I hated it. She didn't say anything more. We just stood there looking at one another. Then I said, "I'll always think well of you, Emily."

She smiled just a little at that. "Thank you, Josh," she answered. Then I turned away. I didn't intend to look back, but I did. And when I waved, she lifted her hand in response. Then she turned and went inside her boxcar room.

I found Joey, and we hunted a long time for Edward C., but we couldn't find a sign of him. Finally we saw Blegan running toward us. He handed me an envelope.

"This is for you from Edward C.," he said in his high childish voice. "He's such a fool—that Edward C. He's off to himself now, bawling because you're leaving. I said to him, 'Good riddance. There's few enough jobs for us who have to wait around for that idiot, Pete Harris, to get things going again.' That's what I said to him. He just kept right on bawling, though, and told me to find you and give you this."

I'm not sure that I thanked Blegan. I took the letter from him, and he was scampering away before I'd had a chance to tear open the envelope. Joey and I read the letter together.

Dear boys, Edward C. had written. *You perhaps will never know what your friendship, your kindness and respect, have meant to a lonely man such as I*

*am. I cannot bear to say good-bye, for I don't want
you to see my tears. My love goes with you.*

> *Your friend,*
> *Edward C. Kensington*

When Joey handed the letter back to me, I
folded it and put it in one of the compartments
my wallet.

We struck out late in the afternoon and caught
two rides before dark, short ones, the two of
them getting us only about twenty miles from
Baton Rouge. Then a truck driver picked us up
and drove us nearly fifty miles farther north. This
driver, unlike Lonnie, talked almost constantly,
sometimes addressing us directly, sometimes
seeming to pour out the words without caring
whether anyone listened or not. Over and over he
talked about the rising mood of anger among the
people, the feeling among the jobless and the
starving that they must rise against men in high
office who could so mismanage a country's econo-
my as to bring us to what we were living through.

"There's going to be a turning point—there's
got to be a turning in the history of this country,"
he said, his voice growing louder and louder. "God
didn't create this unemployment and hunger—
throw it in their teeth if they tell you that. This
misery has been created by men. And the men
who made this are going to be faced with their

work—you wait—they're going to be faced with
their evil."

His voice suddenly broke. We listened in embarrassed silence as he tried to talk in a voice
that choked over his words. "There's going to be
a change, I tell you, or the men that created these
times are not going to be around to see the
change that comes after them."

When he stopped his truck and told us he could
carry us no farther, he put his hand heavily on
my shoulder. "Don't forget," he said harshly,
"never forget what the system has done to you
and thousands more like you. You are the kids
with life in front of you. Don't forget for one
minute that the system has sacrificed the kids of
your generation, you and my kids, and starving
kids all over the nation. Don't forget it. Think
about it, and when you can, do something about
it."

He looked feverish and wild. I was deeply troubled when we left him. There was an urgency in
his voice and manner that left me wondering.

A few days later we happened upon a group of
men who were cooking at a campfire along a
railroad track. They invited us to share the rabbit
stew that bubbled above the fire in an old lard
can—excellent stew, in need of salt, but hot and
nourishing. One man stood like a preacher before
his congregation and spoke to the others; he

talked in a loud, angry voice, and the gist of his words matched the words of the truck driver.

"They call it a democracy, don't they? People starve, people freeze, people tear their hearts out. But they're living in a democracy. And that's enough, isn't it? It's unthinkable, isn't it, to want anything more than a democracy even if under a democracy you're starved and frozen and beaten into the ground? It's unthinkable, is it? Well, I tell you men and you two boys, if a democracy doesn't work, it's got to be junked for something else. And I ask you—you that would work at any job if you could get a chance, you that don't ask for rib roasts but would settle for a little bread, you that somehow got the idea that this was a land of opportunity, I ask you: Is democracy enough? Is it helping to fill the bellies of your hungry children, is it allowing you to hold your head up like a man, is it making you proud of your country? I ask you, is democracy working for *you?*"

The men yelled back. "No, it ain't workin', Tom." "You're right. Democracy ain't doin' a damn thing for us that are down and out."

"Enough of you say that together loud enough and there'll be a change. There'll be a change that will make men in high places run for cover."

He talked on and on. When the meal was finished and the men went their several ways, one man walked with Joey and me for a little distance.

"There's a great anger growing among people," he said as if he were thinking aloud. "People can't take one year of starvation after another with patience. They become angered, and once angered, they begin to question, to think, to demand. This man, Roosevelt, that the people elected in November had better have some answers. He'd better do some hard thinkin' before he takes office next month."

But whether democracy tottered or fell or lifted its head, we had to trudge on. We walked on at times when I wondered if it was possible for two pairs of legs ever to cover the miles before us. There were moments when I asked myself what demon inside me had made it seem sensible to leave a spot where we had a chance of finding comparative comfort and to feel that finding Lonnie was the all-important goal to be followed. I didn't mention my doubts to Joey, though. Instinctively, I knew that as long as he believed I was firm of purpose and confident of being right, he would be firm and confident too. He strode along beside me without a whimper, and I wouldn't take the chance of shattering the resolve that kept his thin shoulders erect even when fatigue made his feet stumble occasionally.

The long trek had gone on for several days when we saw a car such as I hadn't seen since a time when Howie and I watched the funeral procession of a big gangster in Chicago. It was a

136

Cadillac, black and shining, with wooden spoke wheels and lots of polished nickel. It sounded contented and well cared for as it sped along the highway. Joey and I were amazed when the driver stopped and offered us a lift. Quickly, before he could change his mind, we stepped onto the broad running board and into the car. Joey settled in the back, and I sat on the huge front seat, which was upholstered with fabric as soft as a rich woman's dress.

The driver was a very young man, not more than three or four years older than I was. He was a pink, rather fat fellow with a face that looked somewhat like that of an overgrown baby. He introduced himself as "Charley" and added that we were not to bother about his last name. He told us slyly that the car was a "special job," that it cost a cool seven thousand dollars—after it had been fitted with certain little gadgets.

It didn't take long to discover that Charley needed an audience for his boasts. However, he was kind enough in his way, and the comfort of his car made our tired legs tingle with relief.

"Guys in my job can't talk too much," he told us with an important set of his shoulders. "Maybe you've heard of gents ending up stuffed into the trunk of some standard automobile? Well, that could be me, little brothers, so don't ask me any questions because I won't answer them. I know my job too well to run off at the mouth."

We hadn't really intended to ask him any ques-

137

tions; we only wanted a ride, and were delighted by the luxury and comfort we had suddenly found. We were quite willing to sit quietly and enjoy the powerful feel of the big car and to watch the many miles of our journey unfold before us. But Charley was not willing to be quiet; it was plain that he rather intensely wanted to impress us and that the dangers involved in loose talk, which he had just pointed out, became less vivid in his eyes as the urge to brag overcame his fears.

"You have any idea what's in this car?" he asked me finally. The question came out of one side of his mouth at a moment when Joey was curled up in the back seat absorbed in a comic book he had found there.

"No," I said, "not an idea."

He drove several miles without saying anything, but with a little smirk on his mouth. I pretty well knew that he was going to take a hair-raising risk and tell me some professional secret. It was evident that he was like some little kid—getting stuffed into the trunk of a car by unhappy employers could happen to some other fellow; certainly it couldn't possibly happen to him.

Finally he could bear his secret no longer. "Look," he said, "I wouldn't tell you this except I know you're just a kid with no important connections. I'm plenty careful who I talk to, but I reckon I can trust you. Right?"

"Sure," I said, "you can trust me. But use your own judgment. I'm not asking you anything."

"I know you're not. And you had just better not because I've got a way of brushing off people whose noses stretch out too far into my affairs."

We drove on in silence. I watched the mileage meter and made a private bet that he'd tell me his important news before we'd gone ten miles. I was right. It was seven and a half.

"Well, look, little brother, there's a tank under the body of this car, a great big tank that holds over one hundred gallons, liquid measure. Would you have a guess as to what's in it?"

I shook my head. I knew well enough what was in his mysterious tank, but I played the simple peasant.

"Milk?" I asked. "Is this a kind of fancy milk truck?"

That made him laugh pretty hard. It was obvious that his feeling of superiority over a dumb little yokel was making him feel good.

"No, it's not milk, my young friend. It's hooch. The finest, most expensive hooch to make its way into the States down at New Orleans. And you want to know something else? Under that uphol-stery on the doors there are flat containers—nice big flat containers—and they don't hold milk ei-ther." He winked at me and chuckled again. His face was very pink and had a self-satisfied look.

"I run a big risk, of course. That's the reason

they pay me the kind of wages I get." He glanced from his good-looking suit and polished shoes to the outlandish clothes that Pete Harris had given me when I started to work in the carnival. "If I named you the money I'll get for this trip, your mouth would fall open. But it's the risk that gets me the big money."

"The risk of government agents stopping you I suppose?" He didn't seem to realize that I was asking a question; he was feeling too good.

"That's it, little brother; that's the risk. The dirty Feds. But they start chasing me and you know what I do? Any idea?"

"No," I said, knowing that the whole affair was about to be made clear for me.

"Well, sir I get this old Cad up to ninety miles per hour—there ain't a car in the whole government that can match that speed—well, I get it up to ninety, and then I do just one simple thing that makes me innocent like a little idiot lamb." He reached down under the dashboard and drew out a length of cable, very strong and competent-looking. "I just give this cable a quick pull and every drop of hooch in the big tank and in the side ones spills out on the road. Every drop. Nothing left but empty tanks. It's not against the law to have empty tanks in your car if all the hooch is out on the road."

I glanced at the rearview mirror and tried to imagine what it would be like to see a Federal car bearing down upon us.

"Have they chased you often?" I asked, feeling pretty sure that Charley was no longer sensitive to questioning.

"Matter of fact, no. But there's always a first time. I'm expecting it any day. And believe me, little brother, I'm ready for 'em."

"How will you recognize them?" I asked, genuinely interested.

"Hell, you can smell 'em," Charley answered airily.

I felt that answer needed some explanation, but I didn't care to seem too curious. "Must be a pretty exciting job," I said, trying to look envious.

Charley was pleased with me. "It is, my friend. Pretty exciting and pretty dangerous. But then, you want to make big money, you got to take big chances. That's me. I'm not in this game for peanuts. I give you the right to believe that or not."

"Oh, I believe you," I said. I felt I could afford a little buttering up for Charley. After all, Joey and I were getting a wonderful ride, a ride we were enjoying immensely. Once when I glanced back at Joey, he met my look above the top of his comic book and gave me a wink that contorted half his face. It gave me a feeling of satisfaction; Joey and I were nobodies, but we were still able to feel superior to the shallowness of a well-dressed minor hoodlum. We leaned back in the luxury Charley was affording us, relaxed, amused, and complacent.

He drove us the rest of the afternoon, and boasted every mile of the way. He could name us some big names, could Charley, and he did, some of the most notorious names of the liquor transport business in dry America. His watch was a little gift from an uncle whose name was famous; his job had been handed to him on a silver platter by another underworld relative whose name was capable of spreading terror in the hearts of his rivals. Charley had names enough at his command to have carried his stories well into the night, but fortunately when night came, he had to stop at a hotel that had been selected for some reasons of security by his superiors. I would gladly have thanked him and said good-bye when we climbed out of his car, but Charley wouldn't have that; he was taking us to supper.

He left the big car at the hotel, and then the three of us went to a small cafe down the street where Joey and I, with the caution of people who have gone hungry, ordered the cheapest item on the menu and Charley had a sizable steak. I knew I couldn't affort it, but a certain pride, maybe a slight spiritual kinship with Charley, made me feel that since my wallet was stocked with the twenty dollars earned at the carnival, I should pay for his supper in return for the lift he'd given us. But Charley would have none of that. "Not on your life, little brother," he told me. "I got plenty of this folding stuff and more on its way. This two-bit supper is on old Charley."

And so that was settled. After eating we sat at the table for a long time, Joey and I paying for our supper by listening attentively to Charley and being dutifully impressed.

Then Charley drew out his wallet to pay for our meal, and he was put out that he had nothing smaller than a twenty dollar bill. "I hate to give her a twenty for this chicken-feed bill," he said. "but it's the smallest I have." He began searching through all his pockets with some irritation.

The streak that had spurred me to show off by offering to pay for Charley's supper again came to the fore. I didn't like Charley much, I didn't ever expect to see him again, but I somehow had to let him know that I had a wallet too, that I carried big money around with me—just like any gangster-hired flunkie who couldn't keep his mouth shut. I said, "Well, if it's change for a twenty you want, I've got it here." I took out a ten dollar bill, a five, and five singles.

Charley was impressed. "Say, you're doin' all right, little brother." He gave me his twenty with a flourish, took my bills, and left one of them as a tip for the waitress. It amounted to something like fifty percent of the bill. I think she was surprised.

Joey and I left Charley outside the cafe shortly afterward and began to look for a house where we might find a bed for the night. A deep uneasiness began to grow inside me; I noticed that Joey looked grave too. I suddenly wondered if I could offer a twenty dollar bill in payment for a fifty cent bed for the night—which was as much as we could afford to pay.

Joey apparently knew what I was thinking. "I have five singles and three quarters," he said shortly. We had been living so far on the nickels and dimes Joey had collected on the carnival grounds for his singing. I could see he was irritated with me, and I didn't blame him.

In a rundown section of town we found a place where a family would rent a bed for fifty cents. Joey paid for it the next morning, and when we found a cheap cafe farther on, he paid for our breakfast too.

We traveled by foot most of the day, getting only a short ride or two between towns. The weather was getting slightly colder; one man who gave us a lift told us that the northern cold was reaching down into parts of Texas. I glanced at Joey's worn-out shoes and remembered something that had been on my mind when we left the warmth of Louisiana; before we reached snow country, I had to see to it that Joey had warm overshoes. When we got into the town where our driver set us down, I looked around until I found a shoe shop.

It was a dingy little place, partly a cobbler's shop with a few boxes of shoes lined up on one wall. The man who waited on us was a lean, sour-looking character, and there was a kind of smelly, vile air about the shop. However, I was eager to get the overshoes, and because they cost a dollar and a half, I felt that this was a good chance to get my twenty dollar bill changed.

The man gave me a mean look when I handed the bill to him. "This the smallest you got?" he asked.

"Yes," I said. "In fact, it's *all* I've got."

He looked at the bill, folding it together and then smoothing it out. "Where'd you steal this?" he asked curtly.

"I didn't steal it. I've been working for a carnival down in Baton Rouge. This is the money I saved in four weeks."

"Likely story. I aint' seen a kid with this much money on him in two years." He leaned forward suddenly and barked in my face. "Come clear now, where'd you steal this?"

"I've told you I didn't steal it. But if you don't want to do business with me, give me my money and I'll buy overshoes somewhere else."

"Oh, no, you won't." He drew the bill back, then held it up to the light, peering at it from all angles. When a gray rabbitlike man shuffled past the door, the shopkeeper called to him. "Hey, sheriff, come in here a minute."

The man looked dazed. "What you sayin', Alf? What you want with me?"

"I'm tellin' you to come in. What's the matter—you only been elected sheriff so lately you don't recognize your title?"

The man shook his head, frowning as he stood

145

in the doorway. The shopkeeper walked over to him. "Now, sheriff, you've had a lot of experience—I want you to tell me something'. This here is a counterfeit bill, ain't it? Look at it careful and tell me. Come on now, it's counterfeit, ain't it?"

The little gray man swallowed. He glanced at us and back at the man in front of him. "I reckon, if you say so, Alf. I reckon—"

"Not if *I* say so—I want *your* word, sheriff. Right here before these kids. This is a counterfeit bill, ain't it?"

"Yeah. Yeah, I'd say it's counterfeit, Alf. Looks to me like a counterfeit."

"All right. That's all I wanted to know. Thank you, sheriff. You can get on down to the jail now. I may have some customers for you before long."

The man shuffled off, and the shoeman turned to us. "Now, you kids listen to me—one yip out of you and I'll have you turned in for most any misdemeanor I can think of. I can have this young one shut up in a detention home, and you, my friend, you can loll in the county jail for a while and see how you like it. Now, I'm givin' you a chance. You can take the overshoes. I'll do that much for you, but I'm keepin' the bill. I might just turn it in to the government—let 'em go to work trackin' down the counterfeiters. So take your choice—git out with the overshoes or yip just once and see what happens to you."

We were helpless and I knew it. He could tell

almost any lie about us; he could trump up any one of a half dozen stories to get us into trouble, and he could produce a half dozen little rabbit-men who would let themselves be bullied into becoming his accomplices.

I had never wanted to strike another person so much in my life, but I realized that here was real danger. Here was a liar and a thief who had us at his mercy, and he knew it. We picked up the box containing the overshoes and walked out. Joey's face was white; I expect mine was too. I glanced back just once, and the man was looking at us with half-closed eyes and a hateful little smile on his mouth.

We got out of town as quickly as possible; we got out without saying a word to one another. Once out on the highway I glanced at Joey and saw tears all over his face. I was miserable as we walked down the highway together.

Finally I said, "It's my fault, Joey. I had to impress a small-time gangster that I had money in my wallet. We could have paid for your over-shoes with dollar bills and the old man wouldn't have got any big ideas. I'm a stupid fool—there's no doubt about it. I ought to be kicked from here to Omaha."

Joey grinned as he wiped his eyes with the back of his hand. "I'm not goin' to kick you while I'm wearin' my twenty dollar overshoes, little broth-er," he said, mimicking Charley's patronizing tone.

We felt somewhat better because we were able to laugh. I knew it was pointless to dwell on our loss; I tried to get my mind on other things, but the shoeman's meanness and sheer gall would flash back in my mind in spite of myself. Sometimes I clenched my fists and could almost feel the impact of my knuckles against his ugly face.

In spite of our loss we weren't as poor as we had been at times that year. We still had Emily's cookies and the bag of pecans, and Joey had over four dollars in his pockets. A few months earlier we would have felt wealthy with those assets.

Late in the afternoon, after a ten mile lift in a farmer's truck and what must have been a five mile walk on our own, we had a bit of luck in finding a place to sleep. It was a country schoolhouse, and a thin curl of smoke from the chimney told me that a fire had been banked in the stove for the night. I figured if we could get inside we'd have a warm place to rest until morning.

To our surprise the door wasn't locked. The latch was broken, and there had been no attempt made to bar entrance. Once inside we could understand the lack of concern over a lock; there just wasn't anything of value to be taken. There were fifteen or twenty desks, a few of them broken down, all of them ink-covered and scratched. There was an ancient globe, a few dull-looking textbooks, and a stretch of blackboard on which someone, probably a teacher, had written, "Reduce to the lowest common denominator," but

whatever was to have been reduced was erased.
That written command somehow amused me,
sourly and unhappily. I didn't quite know why.

The schoolroom didn't look like much. I could
imagine how kids hated being there. We poked
around for a while, but there wasn't much to see;
besides, we were dead tired, and so we pulled a
couple of desks up to the big stove and stretched
our legs out toward the warmth. We took out
four of Emily's cookies and handful of pecans for
our supper, and while we ate, we talked about one
thing and another, both of us avoiding the painful
subject of our humiliation in the shoe shop. Then
as darkness filled the room, we wrapped ourselves
in the blanket Emily had given us and made the
dusty floor our bed for the night.

We slept heavily in spite of anger and worry. I
woke up when the first light of morning began
drifting in and got up quietly to stand at one of
the grimy windows. I looked out at the morning
for a long time, trying to think straight.

I tried to make plans as I stood there. With
Joey's money we could eat a little for a few days;
with luck we could catch a few long rides during
the day and find a few warm spots where we
could rest at night. It surely wouldn't be too long
until we'd reach Nebraska, and Nebraska meant
Lonnie and Lonnie meant comfort and protection.
Even as that thought came to me, however, I
realized that Joey and I could not knock at Lonnie's door some morning and say, "Here we are.

Be a father to us." I was not quite that childish. Somehow we had to show him that we were able to get along, that our need for him was only a need for friendship. In the back of my mind, though, I knew that it was the need of two kids who were fearful of a black abyss which they might have to face alone.

Joey stirred restlessly in half-wakeful sleep. "Will we have any breakfast, Josh?" he asked.

I couldn't answer for a moment; then I called to him, telling him we'd better be getting on our way, that maybe we'd find something to eat farther down the road.

We had breakfast in the next little town. I made Joey eat an egg and toast and drink a cup of hot cocoa. I had only cocoa after I'd convinced Joey that I wasn't hungry. A guy who could help bring about the loss of twenty dollars as I had done, could simply pull his belt a little tighter.

We walked long distances during the next few weeks, getting a lift now and then, usually in some farmer's truck. Occasionally we got a fifty-mile ride, and on two or three red-letter days we were treated to a hot dog or a chocolate bar by some kindly driver. We found places to sleep— a hallway in the business section of a town, a railroad depot, a haystack on a mild night; a few times some families let us have a bed for a quarter, but as Joey's money dwindled, we saved every cent for food which was more important than a bed.

As the winds grew harsher and the snow deeper, I worried about Joey. The bitter February weather we encountered as we moved into Kansas was a threat to anyone as undernourished and over-tired as we were. Surprisingly enough, however, Joey's health was better than mine. I developed a deep cough that grew worse with each day, and it was Joey who spent his last dime to buy cough medicine for me; it was Joey who begged at kitchen doors and brought food to me at times when my legs refused to go any farther.

The business of keeping alive became harder each day. We kept our spirits up by reminding ourselves that we were getting nearer and nearer to Lonnie; that was true, but we were paying a steep price for the fulfillment of our goal.

Chapter Eight

We got to Nebraska the last week in February, exhausted, penniless, and hungry. Joey tried to pick up a few coins by singing and accompanying his songs on the banjo, but icy winds made his fingers numb and the problems of people in general made them hurry past him without paying much attention to the plea that promoted his singing. He did get one windfall, though. in the gift of some beef bones from a kindly butcher who heard Joey's songs and helped him in the kind of coin a butcher could afford.

It was a precious gift, and we eagerly hunted one of the shabbiest houses we could locate—we tended to seek out people as shabby as we were—and we had the good fortune to meet an old man

who agreed to boil the bones on his cookstove for
a share of the soup. He was a gentle old man,
very quiet and sometimes seeming a little dazed.
He asked us no questions, but he frowned when I
had a particularly hard coughing spell; later he
picked up the broken shoes which I had taken off
to dry in front of the fire, and he spent a long
time fitting cardboard soles inside them. When we
were leaving, he gave me a pair of heavy gray
socks and in the quavering voice of aged people,
warned me about keeping my feet dry.

We asked directions many times, and every day
we moved a little farther toward Omaha. I was
burning with fever as we trudged on, but I didn't
let Joey know about that or about how much my
lungs hurt. I suppose he just thought that I was
mean when I snapped at him or ignored his questions. I should have told him how sick I was, but I
didn't.

We stopped one noon at a tar-paper shack near
the railroad tracks, and Joey asked the woman
who came to the door if she could give us something to eat. I said nothing, but as I looked at her,
it occurred to me that her face was burning with
fever too. Her eyes were red and watery, and
there were bright red fever spots on her cheeks.
She was terribly thin and feeble-looking; I almost
knew that we had chosen the wrong place to beg.

The woman screamed at Joey as if he had committed some crime in asking for something to
keep us alive. "What would you have me do?" she

153

asked in a high, wild sort of voice. "Would you have me hand out food to every tramp when my own children have just one meal a day? Do you think I can stretch the little I have to feed tramp-children and see my own starve tomorrow?"

It was dreadful to watch her, to listen to her. The feverish brightness in her eyes made her look like a madwoman. Then as we stood there, not knowing what to say or do, she began to sob in the awful hysterical way Florinda had sobbed on the night of the fire.

I turned away, feeling some pity for her but more anger. "Just a plain *No* would be plenty to get rid of us, lady," I muttered. "You needn't go into details."

But Joey was different. He went up to her and spoke in a low voice. "It's all right," he told her. "We know how hard times are."

She pulled her apron up and hid her face in it, but Joey and I could hear her sobs as we walked down the snowy street. The experience shook us; we knew we had to try again at some other house, but the wildness of the woman we'd just left made us dread to ask anyone else.

We had just turned a corner at the end of the block when I heard her coming down the street and calling to us in the same hysterical voice. I wanted to run from her, but I couldn't. We waited as she came up to us, bareheaded and without a coat in the freezing wind.

"You must come back; you're hungry children,

and I've sinned against others as unfortunate as
my own. I can't rest tonight if I have to remember that I've denied children because they aren't
my own." She was pulling at Joey's arm, but she
seemed to be pleading with me. "You've got to
listen. You must come back. Please. We'll stretch
our meal to help fill all of us."

I didn't want to go back with her, but I was
almost afraid to refuse. She looked so desperate,
so determined that we free her from her feeling
of guilt. And so we thanked her and walked soberly back to the shack where children were
standing at the windows gazing out at their mother and the two strange boy-tramps.

Inside the kitchen we sat at a bare table with
six children lined up beside us. Quickly, the woman lifted the lid from a kettle of soup and poured
more water inside. She had stopped crying, but
she talked to herself in a strange way as she
ladled the soup out into bowls. "We will eat," she
kept repeating. "We will eat, all of us. My hungry
children will eat and another woman's hungry
children too. We will eat today, and maybe the
Lord will provide for tomorrow."

When we left the woman's house, we followed
the railroad tracks to the outskirts of town. Near
the tracks we found a deserted shed and an empty
oil drum in which we built a fire. I told Joey I
thought we'd better rest for a day or two before
going any farther; privately I wondered if I would

155

ever be able to get myself out on the highway
again.

The next day I was too weak to get up, so Joey
went out begging alone. He had real luck at one
house. A woman gave him a whole loaf of bread,
fresh and brown from the oven. I was drowsy
with fever when he brought the loaf in to show
me, but as I fell asleep, I felt a kind of satisfaction
that the bread would provide us with food for the
next few days.

When I woke up, Joey was gone, and it was
nearly dark when he returned. "You know the
lady that gave us the soup—the one that cried so
hard?" he asked. "Well, I took half of our bread
to her. She was so happy she said to thank—" He
stopped, frightened and amazed, I suppose, as I
lurched toward him.

"You gave away our bread, you little fool?
Here we are starving and you give away food
enough to keep us alive for days—"

"She gave *us* food, don't forget that," Joey said
gruffly, moving away from me.

"She gave us a bowl of thin soup. And I don't
care if she gave us beefsteak—we need that
bread. You march yourself right back and tell her
we have to have it." I hardly knew what I was
saying. There was just a burning anger inside me;
no reason, no feeling of compassion or pity.

Joey's thin face was hard as he faced me. "You
can yell at me till you're blue, and a lot of good it
will do you. It was *my* bread, and I had a right to

do what I pleased with it. And I'm not mean enough to forget people that have been good to me even if you are."

Joey didn't know how sick I was. He didn't know. If he had only known, he would have handled me differently. But he didn't. He didn't know.

I struck Joey. It was the first time in my life I'd ever struck him. When I was little, I had been jealous sometimes and resentful, but I'd never laid a hand on him roughly. During the months we'd been on the road, I had come to love him more than anyone else in the world. But as he stood before me, defiant and angry, I forgot the years of training in decent behavior that I had received when I was young. The fever, the feeling of desperation, the red rage—all these things got the better of me. In that blind minute I struck a frail boy five years younger than I was, a boy who had once fed a hungry cat on a night that now seemed a hundred years away, a boy who had given a half loaf of bread to a woman and her hungry children.

Joey fell and I froze in a kind of agony at what I had done. I stood there staring at him on the ground, still staring when he leaped back to his feet and faced me with blazing eyes.

Joey was not at a loss for words. "I've taken a lot from you, Josh, and this is the last. I'm through with you. I'm through right now and for as long as I live. I can take care of myself, and as

157

far as I'm concerned, you can go to the Devil." He grabbed his coat and the banjo; it was strange that I should notice it at such a time, but I felt glad that he was wearing his overshoes. When he went outside, he banged the door of the shed.

I don't know how long I stood there. The fever brought strange patterns to my mind, thoughts that spun in circles, repeating themselves over and over as each circle was completed. "My brother is gone, my brother is gone," whirled through my brain. And then, "Lowest common denominator, lowest common denominator, reduced to the lowest common denominator."

When I opened the door, the twilight had become night. I think I called Joey several times; at least I tried to call him. Then I stumbled out and across the fields in a blind search for him. The half loaf of bread lay on the floor beside the oil drum we had used as a stove.

I had no plan of search for Joey, no sense of direction. I just struck out blindly and kept going except when a seizure of coughing threatened to tear my chest wide open. Whenever that happened, I'd lean against a tree or a fence until I was able to go on. Sometimes I'd think I saw a little figure that looked like Joey in the distance, and I'd run toward it only to find it was some stationary object that suggested a boy's form in the darkness.

"He'll come back—he'll get over his mad spell and come back," I commenced to tell myself after

I'd searched for a long time. I decided I'd better go back to the shed, better be there when Joey got back. "I'll apologize," I repeated over and over again. "I'll make it right with Joey."

I tried for a long time to find the shed again, but I was lost. There was only black night around me and snow that had melted a little during the day and was now a shallow river of slush with a thin layer of freezing crust on the surface. My shoes were filled with water; neither the cardboard soles which the old man had fitted for me nor the heavy socks he'd given me were of any use in keeping out the snow and water.

Panic hit me finally when neither the shed nor Joey could be found. There wasn't a single lighted window in sight, not a doorway where I could find shelter. I coughed so hard that I finally lost my balance and fell. The effort to get up again was too much. "I guess I'm going to die," I thought, and stopped trying to do anything about it.

I had heard that one's whole life passes before his eyes at such a time, but one segment of mine is all that I remember seeing. I seemed to go back to a time when I was a little boy, sick with croup or some childhood ailment. I was lying in Dad's lap with my head against his shoulder, and he was rocking me in the big leather chair that Mom kept in front of the stove in winter. His arms felt strong and comforting; he patted my back rhythmically as he rocked, and he sang to me, an old Polish song of his own childhood. I could feel the

159

vibration of his deep voice when I placed my hand
against his chest. That was all there was to the
memory. After that the light in my brain was
turned out.

Voices came after a while, voices that sounded
a thousand miles away. I had a sensation of being
moved, of wet shoes and socks being taken off,
and of warmth enveloping me. Once I thought I
could feel wheels beneath me and could hear the
sound of them on the road. Then I gave up and
knew nothing at all.

When I woke up, I was in a bed with warm
blankets covering me. There was winter sunshine
coming in through the windows, and the
fragrance of a rich, meaty soup was in the air.
When a coughing fit hit me, the hand and arm of
a man appeared; my head was lifted, and the
hand placed a spoonful of sweet, tangy medicine
between my lips. I swallowed, and the coughing
stopped for a while.

Everything was silent except for the crackle of
fire in a big stove that took up one end of the
room. I was puzzled about where I was, but too
tired and weak to care very much. I knew that
someone was sitting beside me, someone whose
hand and arm had lifted my head and given me
medicine. Someone was kind.

A girl came and stood at the foot of my bed,
a girl in a loose shirt that hung down almost to
her knees. She had stiff brown braids that stuck
out over her ears, and a square little face with a

No Promises in the Wind

few freckles. "Kind of a homely kid," I thought, and was immediately ashamed of my secret unkindness. The girl was studying me soberly.

"I think he's coming back, Lonnie," she said. "Maybe we'd better try to get some more soup down him."

She had said "Lonnie." A flash of joy went through me. I turned my head enough to look up at the man who sat beside me, and before my eyes could focus upon him, I went through some seconds of agony for fear that I hadn't heard right. But I had. Lonnie was beside me, and he nodded, smiling, as I looked up at him.

"You're feeling better, aren't you, Josh? You've had us plenty scared, d'you know it?"

It must have been a long time since I had spoken. I found it hard to form the words I wanted to say. Finally I managed to whisper, "How did you find me?"

"A couple found you at the side of the road in a town about fifty miles south of Omaha. You had my name and address in your wallet so they got in touch with me. Janey and I drove over and brought you home with us."

The girl smiled at me just a little. She was Janey I supposed. But she didn't matter. Some deep trouble within me was trying to push into my mind. I couldn't think what it was, but it was bad. I looked from the girl back to Lonnie.

He leaned down so that his eyes were level with mine. "I know you're too weak to talk much, but

161

there's one thing I've got to know: Where's your brother, Josh? Where's Joey?"

Then it all came back like a big wave sweeping in, all the pain and the meanness that made me strike Joey; the rage in his eyes came back to me and his defiance. I remembered the slush that filled my shoes and the moment when I decided that I couldn't go any farther. I closed my eyes as the memories poured back.

"Tell me, Josh." That was Lonnie again. "Tell me what happened. Then we'll let you sleep again."

The girl's voice was full of sympathy. "He can't talk, Lonnie. Something is hurting him. Don't try to make him talk now."

"I have to know. I have to know right away." He walked over to the stove and ladled some soup into a bowl. Then he handed the bowl to the girl while he lifted my head. "Here, I'll hold his head up; you feed him a little more soup. Maybe it will give him strength."

The tightness in my throat overcame the hunger in me, and I tried to push the spoon away. But Lonnie was determined. "Swallow this soup, Josh. It will make you feel better. Swallow it, I tell you, and make up your mind that you have to talk."

And so I did. I swallowed some of the soup which at another time I would have appreciated as being delicious. At that moment, though, it was tasteless. But Lonnie was right. It gave me strength almost immediately.

When I was able, I told him enough of the story to let him understand what had happened. Lonnie interrupted now and then. He wanted to know if Joey had a cold like mine when he left. He asked about clothing—did Joey have a warm coat? I told him about the overshoes, and that pleased him. At the end I was so tired that I had to whisper the last sentence. I said, "If Joey is gone for good, I don't want to live anymore."

Lonnie was silent for a long time. "I know," he said finally. Then he added in a voice that was suddenly different, very brisk and cheerful. "But he's not gone for good. He's probably doing all right for himself—people can't resist Joey. And we'll find him if we have to take a fine-tooth comb to the state of Nebraska."

He drew a shade down so that the room was in shadow. "Go back to sleep now, Josh. You've got to get a lot of rest. Don't worry. I'll take care of everything."

I believed him. My confidence in him and my weariness made me forget the despair for a while. I went off into a sleep that must have lasted for hours.

When I opened my eyes again, the room was lighted dimly by a kerosene lamp on the table. The girl was gone, and Lonnie was sitting beside the stove, leaning forward with his head in his hands. When I called his name softly, he came over and sat beside me again.

"I feel better, Lonnie."

"Good. You'll come out of this. You must have an iron-plated constitution."

"I want to tell you—I won't stay long. I don't want to be a drag on you."

"You'll stay till you're good and well. That's the way I want it."

"Did you find another job, Lonnie?"

"Yes, I was lucky. I'm not getting rich, but my family is eating. That's something these days."

"Is the girl your family?" I remembered that he'd spoken of a girl—a girl who should have called him Uncle Lonnie but was too set in her ways.

"Yes. Janey's my niece. She's been with us since she was four; her parents were killed in an automobile accident. She and my mother—her gramma—live next door. I look after them. They're all I have."

"She's a nice girl." I felt sorry about that first thought that called her homely.

"That's right. She's a good little kid." He straightened the covers over me and smoothed my pillow. "She'll look in on you once in a while during the day when I'm gone, she and Gramma. They'll see that you get your medicine and are well fed."

We didn't speak for a while. Then I asked what

was foremost in my mind. "Lonnie, do you think we'll find Joey?"

"I'm pretty sure we will. He can't be too far away. It's only three days since we picked you up; he can't travel very far in three days. I notified the police this afternoon while you were asleep. They're looking for him in Omaha and Lincoln—in the smaller towns in this area too. We'll find him. That little squirt can't shake us like this. He's getting too big for his britches."

"He had a right to leave me, Lonnie. I was mean. I don't know what made me do what I did. But Joey didn't understand. He didn't know how sick I was."

"I guess not." Lonnie was looking at me thoughtfully. He nodded as if agreeing with some private thought. Then he slowly wound an alarm clock and prepared to go into his bedroom. "Do everything you can to regain your strength, Josh. And don't worry. I'm going to find that boy for you."

I lay awake for the rest of the night thinking about Joey, wondering and hoping. I wondered if the time would ever come when I could have peace of mind again.

Lonnie was gone when I woke up the next morning, but his mother came over and fixed breakfast for me, washed me, and gave me my medicine. She was kind, but a quiet and rather grim-looking old lady. I found that she was almost deaf which made her seem more remote

than she possibly was by nature. She left as soon
as she had made me comfortable, and I was alone
until Janey came over bringing a small radio with
her.

She looked different. She was still wearing the
loose shirt and blue denim pants that must sometime have belonged to a boy, but her hair wasn't
braided as it had been the night before; it hung
loose, tied back with a red ribbon. It looked nice,
bright brown and bouncy with curls at the ends.
Her cheeks were flushed when she said hello, and
the soft color kind of played down the freckles.
Actually she looked pretty nice. She made me
realize that I must look like a tramp, and at first I
was self-conscious and embarrassed.

She put the radio down on a table near my bed.
"I'm supposed to listen to Mr. Roosevelt's inaugu-
ral address—my civics teacher gave us this for an
assignment. I thought maybe you'd like to hear it
too."

I had forgotten about elections and presidents
and inaugurations. For months I hadn't thought
about much of anything except where we'd find
food for the next meal, where we'd be able to
sleep without freezing. I didn't for one minute
suppose that anything happening in Washington,
D.C., might in any way affect my problems. But
this was the fourth of March, 1933, and I was
willing to listen to anything that would take my
mind off Joey for the moment.

The announcer was describing the scene in

Washington when Janey tuned in the station. The day was gray and bleak out there, he told us, but in spite of the chill wind there were nearly a hundred thousand people on the streets and the grounds around the Capitol. It was a crowd of tired and grim faces—I could well believe that—a crowd amazingly quiet for such a huge gathering.

He described the procession coming down Pennsylvania Avenue—there was the car carrying the outgoing president, Mr. Hoover, and the president-elect, Mr Roosevelt. "President Hoover's face is stern and unsmiling," the announcer said. "He doesn't wave or pay any attention to the crowds."

"People have been rough on President Hoover," Janey told me quietly. "They blame him for everything. You know very well that no one man could have made all this mess. Why do they have to pin it all on Mr. Hoover?"

I shook my head, hoping she would be quiet so that I could hear more. The announcer went on, "Those near him say that Mr. Roosevelt seems preoccupied with his thoughts. He and Mr. Hoover are not conversing; the president-elect seems to share President Hoover's attitude of brooding."

We listened for a long time to the announcer's description of the scene. Then, at last, he told us excitedly that Mr. Roosevelt was walking slowly down a ramp, leaning on the arm of his son for support. "He's crippled, you know," Janey whispered to me. "Lots of people don't realize it because he never talks about it, or acts as if he's any different. But he is. Polio. He can't walk alone."

The announcer's voice had become very tense. "The Marine Band has just finished playing 'Hail to the Chief,' " he said in a low, but excited voice. "Charles Evans Hughes, chief justice of the Supreme Court, is awaiting Mr. Roosevelt's approach to the lectern—gray, splendid old Mr. Hughes, who was himself so nearly president in 1916—"

"Did you know that?" Janey asked me, her voice excited too. "People were actually saying 'President Hughes,' and then the last votes came in that elected Woodrow Wilson."

Finally she was quiet, and I could hear the announcer again. "The wind is blowing Mr. Hughes's white hair—Mr. Roosevelt is very pale he is at the lectern now—he is placing his right hand on the Bible—"

I felt tense and strangely moved. Maybe it was because I was weak, but as I heard the strange voice, so different from the voices I had heard all my life—when I heard that voice repeat the oath of office after Chief Justice Hughes, I felt tears come into my eyes. The unfamiliar words had a sonorous ring: "I, Franklin Delano Roosevelt, do solemnly swear—that I will faithfully execute the office of the President of the United States—and will, to the best of my ability—preserve, protect, and defend the Constitution of the United States so help me God."

Janey pretended not to notice that I was deeply moved. She sat like a boy, astride a chair with her hands clasped loosely over the chair's back. "All right, Mr. Roosevelt," she muttered, "I made Lonnie vote for you. Now let's see what you can do."

The new president was speaking. "This is a day of national consecration . . ." he said. I wondered what Mr. Hoover was thinking. I went on listening, not understanding all of what he said, then suddenly aware of something that seemed very personal to me. " . . . the only thing we have to fear is fear itself—nameless, unreasoning, unjustified terror—"

"Not unjustified, Mr. President," I thought. "The terror has not been unjustified. *You* don't know."

Then back to the speech. "The Nation asks for action, and action now. . . . We must move as a trained and loyal army, willing to sacrifice for the good of a common discipline—"

Janey jotted down a few notes to take to class on Monday, and we listened until the speech was finished. Then she snapped off the radio and looked at me. "Well, what do you think?"

"I didn't understand all of it," I said, "but what I understand makes me hope a little. It seems that he has plans, that he's going to do something about the trouble we're going through."

169

"When Lonnie talks to me about Roosevelt, he says, 'Maybe—with a capital *M* and a question mark.' Lonnie's not sure. But me—I've got a lot of confidence in the man. I don't know why, but I just have a feeling he's going to do some good for us."

She looked so funny—so half-plain and boyish, so half-pretty and girlish. Her face was very serious. "I wish I could help him. I wish I was a woman and he'd ask me to join his cabinet. I'd like to pitch in and help him get things really moving." She looked at me suspiciously. "You think I'm some kind of a nut, don't you?"

"No, I don't. Honest I don't."

"You were smiling. It's the first time I've seen you smile."

"I guess I'm just naturally a little sober-looking."

"You're like Lonnie. He's sober-looking too, but he always grins when I get excited over politics."

"That's because most girls your age don't think much about politics."

She nodded. "I know. Most of the kids in my class think I'm an oddball."

"I don't supose many girls tell their uncles how to vote, do they?"

She grinned at me a little sheepishly. "*That* was something of a slight exaggeration," she admitted.

"But Lonnie does do just about what you tell him to do, I'll bet."

"Just about," she agreed, her lips pursed slightly. "Gram says I wind him around my finger, but I don't. I don't want to dominate people. I just like to *convince* them."

That made me laugh. It seemed so long since I had laughed that I was surprised at myself. Janey looked pleased.

"You're lots better," she commented.

"You make me feel lots better," I told her.

That made her blush deeply, but she didn't act skittish or silly. She just sat there studying me for a minute. Then she said, "Lonnie had a boy once. The night we drove over to pick you up, he told me that you're exactly the age Davy would have been."

I didn't feel that I should talk about Lonnie's boy so I said nothing. After a while she continued. "I loved Davy so much—and Aunt Helen. She was just about a real mother to me. After Davy died, she was never the same, though. She didn't seem to love me the way she used to, and I guess something happened between her and Lonnie. Gram won't talk about it, and I sure don't ask Lonnie things that are none of my business. I think about Aunt Helen, though, and I get a deep, lonesome feeling for her sometimes."

We talked for a long time that afternoon. She gave me medicine when I coughed a lot, and saw to it that the fire kept going so that the room stayed warm. She was more than a year younger than I was, and in some ways she seemed as

171

young as Joey; then again at times she might have been older than I was.

We played two games of checkers at which she beat me unmercifully the first time and rather obviously allowed me to win the second time. After that she read aloud—the newspaper mostly, and her voice was nice. I closed my eyes and listened for a long time; then I slept, and when I woke up, she was at the stove fixing something for supper.

As I watched her, I thought of Emily. She was not as beautiful as Emily, not anywhere nearly as beautiful. Still there was something about her that was warm and friendly. I wondered idly if I'd ever fall in love with Janey. I didn't think so, but I found myself wondering. I said, "Janey, do you ever wear earrings?"

She didn't even turn to look at me as she answered. "I'd feel like a fool in 'em," she said shortly. That seemed to settle things. The girl that I loved would have to wear earrings.

Then I thought of Joey, and such things as earrings and girls, even Lonnie and security, all seemed less than nothing.

Chapter Nine

I lay awake night after night during that time of convalescence, hurting at thoughts about Joey. I tried to think of other things, tried to tell myself that of course Lonnie would be able to find Joey, that we'd get things smoothed over, that we'd find a place where we'd be safe and comfortable together. I tried to make plans for our future, Joey's and mine, but it was no good. Memories crowded in to make me lonely and depressed. I thought of Joey and Howie down at the corner of Randolph and Wabash in Chicago's Loop, Joey singing a little off-key now and then, Howie playing the banjo and grinning at Joey as if they were carefree and well-fed, as if they were just having a lark before they went home to security and a good warm supper. My memories darted here and there: Joey giving me a big wink from the back seat of Charley's Cadillac, Joey beaming at Emily when he handed her our box of dimes, Joey's eyes blazing at me that last night when he told me I was mean and could go to the Devil.

Every evening when Lonnie came home my eyes asked him the same question; I didn't need to put that question into words. And every evening he shook his head, the discouragement he felt showing in his face and the slump of his body. He checked the detention homes—someone might have discovered that Joey was on his own and have turned him over to the local authorities. He checked with the police in every town within a radius of fifty miles. They hadn't found a trace of Joey.

"He may have hitchhiked back home," Lonnie speculated one night. "There are a lot of trucks leaving here for Chicago. It would have been a smart thing for him to do—and Joey's smart. That just may be the answer."

I didn't believe it. I couldn't argue too strongly that Joey still loved me, but somehow I was convinced he was looking for me, that he would have refused to run home like a frightened little boy, admitting he'd broken with me and couldn't make it alone. This was not Joey's way, though for his own safety I might have wished that it was. However, Lonnie was firm about following up every possibility, and so I gave him our home address
174

and he spent a long time that evening in writing a letter.

Janey often helped me out of my dark moods, coming over to see me almost every afternoon. Toward three o'clock I'd listen eagerly for the bang of the front door in the house next to Lonnie's, a bang that meant Janey was home from school. Then a short time later—just the time it took for her to discard her school dress and get into something more to her liking—she would appear, slender and agile, in boyish clothes, her pretty hair blowing in the wind. She would come running into the kitchen where I lay, sometimes with hot rolls fresh from Gramma's oven, sometimes with crackers and peanut butter, and we'd eat together and have glasses of milk or the remainder of the morning cocoa that Lonnie left on the stove for us.

She made me talk, whether I wanted to or not. She wanted to know about my music, she questioned me about the things that had happened to Joey and me since we left home, she wanted to know all about Kitty, about Howie, about Edward C. She would draw up a chair beside my bed, sitting astride it and listening attentively to everything I told her.

One afternoon as she sat beside me she drummed her fingers thoughtfully on the back of the chair, and when I stopped talking, she was silent too. Then suddenly she slid to the floor and

175

sat cross-legged there, her face on a level with mine.

"What did you mean by that remark about earrings the first afternoon we talked together, Josh?" she asked.

"I don't know. Just a silly idea," I answered. I had never mentioned Emily to her.

"Come on. You knew someone pretty who wore earrings, didn't you?"

"Yes. But she wasn't a girl like you; she was a woman in the carnival down in Louisiana."

"Did you love her, Josh?"

I didn't answer right away. Then I said, "In a way I guess—I'm not sure. Maybe I was just lonely."

She made little pleats in the loose end of a blanket that fell on the side of my bed; then she smoothed out the pleats and made them all over again.

"People—boys, that is—don't love girls unless they're pretty, do they, Josh?"

"I don't know much about love and—and girls, Janey. But you don't have to worry about how you look."

She was thoughtful for a minute; then she sighed. "I tried on some earrings in the dime store this noon, Josh. I was right—they looked silly on me."

She seemed awfully young to me at that moment. I wanted to be kind to her, kind the way Emily had been to me. "You don't need earrings,

176

Janey. You're sweet and nice—and you're pretty too. I guess it's just older women who need earrings."

She grew very red when I said that to her. I liked the blush that spread over her face and even to the part of her neck where her shirt collar lay open. But I could see that she felt awkward and self-conscious—she was no longer the poised little tomboy who talked about organized labor and how a man named Herbert Spence had felt about government aid for the poor. She looked much more like an unhappy little kid who didn't know what to do next. I felt very tender toward Janey at that moment, and because I wanted to reassure her, I stretched out my hand to hers. When our hands met, she lifted mine and pressed her cheek against it.

She left abruptly after that and didn't return until she and Gramma came over to prepare supper. We always ate, to tell the truth, considerably better when Gramma helped to cook the meal than when Janey did it alone. It was an especially good supper; Lonnie talked more than usual, and even Gramma smiled a little now and then. Once she pointed her finger at me and said, "Now if my girl gets to be a nuisance running over here every afternoon, you tell me and I'll keep her at home."

Lonnie glanced at me quickly and then at Janey. We had been very quiet, both of us, and at Gramma's words I guess each of us became very red. I noticed that when Janey brought the

177

coffeepot over to refill Lonnie's cup, he put his
arm around her waist and drew her to his side.
She leaned down and kissed his forehead lightly.
It almost seemed as if they said something to one
another in those two gestures.

That night when we were alone Lonnie and I
talked for a long time. We talked about Joey and
the plans Lonnie was going to carry out if we
found that my brother had not gone home. Lonnie seemed hopeful as we talked things over.

"At least we can pretty well rule out death by
starvation or freezing. There's been no little blond
boy found dead, thank God, in any of the towns
where I have contacts. I don't think Joey would
have gone much farther west; if he had a mind to
get out of this part of the country, he'd head for
Chicago and home."

"Would he have tried to go back south, do you
think? He liked Pete Harris and Edward C. and—
and Emily. He might have decided to go back
down there."

"I'm in touch with Harris," Lonnie answered.
"If Joey turns up down there, Harris will let us
know. He was pretty well worked up when I told
him about Joey."

"You made a long distance call to Baton Rouge,
Lonnie?" I asked incredulously. My debt to him
seemed to be growing fast. I wondered how I
could ever repay it.

"Keep your shirt on—it wasn't too bad. Anyway, we're going to find that boy no matter what

it costs, no matter if the rest of us have to live on beans."

I sat up in the big rocking chair until bedtime. Lonnie pulled me up near the stove and sat astride one of the kitchen chairs.

"Janey likes to sit like that," I said, smiling. I hadn't intended to mention her name, but I forgot.

"She learned that from me. She's always aped me since she was knee-high—she and the boy too." He leaned forward and closed a damper on the stove. "She's got to begin wearing dresses more and sitting like a lady now that she's growing up. I must have a talk with her."

"She's a very intelligent girl," I said weakly because it was not Janey's intelligence that I was thinking about. I was still remembering the feel of her soft cheek against my hand.

Lonnie leaned forward resting his chin on the back of his chair. "She's pretty fond of you, isn't she, Josh?"

"I don't know. Maybe. I know I like *her*. Is that all right?"

He took that long deep breath I had noticed once before when it had struck me that he felt some weight inside his chest. His voice was cheerful, though, when he answered.

"Yes, it's all right. Of course it's all right. You're both getting to an age when it's easy to be fond of one another. Sure. It's natural and right. It's just one of those things, I guess. Makes me

179

remember when I first allowed Davy to cross the street by himself and find his own way to kindergarten. I knew it had to be, but it wasn't easy." He paused a minute and then continued, "I have a lot of respect for you, Josh; I like you. If I didn't, I wouldn't let Janey spend so much time over here."

"Yes. I know what you mean," I answered.

"You're over a year older than Janey. She's never gone out with boys yet. You probably are a little more experienced in this business of dating."

I laughed shortly. "I've never had a girl in my life. I've always been afraid of them. It's nice not to be afraid of Janey."

"What about the young lady down at the carnival—the one with the earrings?"

"Janey told you about that?"

"She mentioned it. She wanted to know if she could have a little money to buy some dime store earrings. That was because Josh had known a pretty girl at the carnival who wore them."

I didn't say anything. We sat there for a while.

"You don't care to talk about the girl at the carnival?"

"I'd rather not," I answered.

"All right, then, we won't." He smiled and got to his feet. "You'd better get to bed—we don't want you to get over-tired. You're still a little on the wobbly side."

The next few days were much the same except

that Janey wore dresses when she came over to
see me and she sat on the chair in what I supposed Lonnie had told her was a ladylike manner.
We talked about lots of things, but we never mentioned earrings or love or a girl's smooth cheek
pressed against a boy's hand.

Every day I watched for the mailman, hoping
for a letter from home, knowing guiltily that I
didn't deserve one after all the weeks in which I
had refused to write. But there was one thing I
had to know even if I had to write and plead for a
letter: I had to know if they had heard from
Joey. More and more I leaned toward Lonnie's
idea that Joey might have gone home; more and
more I hoped that idea was right.

"Maybe they'll never forgive me," I thought.
"All right, I can take it. I can take anything if only
I know that Joey is safe with them—if only I know
idea that Joey might have gone home; more and
shelter."

The letter came one stormy afternoon when I
was alone. It was addressed to Lonnie in Mom's
handwriting. I sat there in the quiet kitchen waiting for Lonnie to get home, turning the envelope
over and over in my hands, seeing in my mind the
room at home and the table where Mom must
have sat as she wrote.

Janey was with me by the time Lonnie came
home for supper, and we stood together, hardly
breathing as he tore the envelope open. There was
an enclosed letter which he handed to me. I

clutched it as I listened to Lonnie read what Mom had written to him.

They had not heard from Joey since we left Baton Rouge. She told Lonnie that she watched every mail hoping to hear from one of us, but that it seemed as if a great darkness had gobbled both of us up. She thanked him for taking care of me during my sickness, and she begged him to let her know as soon as we had any word from Joey. Lonnie reread a part of the letter to himself; then he folded it slowly and shook his head as he placed it in his coat pocket.

When I unfolded the letter Mom had directed to me, Lonnie found an excuse for him and Janey to leave the kitchen and allow me to be alone. When they were gone, I just sat there in the half-darkness, holding the letter tightly, wanting to read it and yet afraid I couldn't bear what she might have to say.

Finally I turned on the light bulb that hung from the kitchen ceiling and spread the closely written page out in front of me.

She asked me first to believe that she loved me and that she would never be happy until Joey and I were home. After that she talked about Dad. I wouldn't know him, she said; he looked like an old man what with worry and anxiety and remorse for his boys. He had a job of sorts—not a good one and not steady, but it had saved his sanity, she thought.

Kitty had a job typing in an office down in the

Loop; she sent her love to me and begged me to find Joey and come home. "Your sister loves you dearly, Josh. She suffers with Dad and me when we have no word from you."

When she told me of *her* job, there was almost a hint of laughter in the paragraph—laughter had come so easily to her in the old days.

"Your mother is getting mixed up with some of the ruder elements of Chicago, dear boy. I answered an ad in the paper, and I am now giving music lessons to the wife of one of the city's west side gangsters. She's a quiet and pretty young woman, but she has very little aptitude for music. I think she is lonely and perhaps frightened. It is plain that she is paying for my company rather than for my teaching, but she has been very generous and kind. She has found five other pupils for me, and the money is a godsend. . . ."

At the end of her letter she said, "Your dad has not had a full night's sleep since you left, Josh. I beg you for his sake and mine to forgive and try to understand all that has happened. Without that forgiveness and understanding, neither Dad nor I will ever know happiness again."

I had read the letter for a third time when Lonnie and Janey came back to the kitchen. It was raining harder than ever by then, a downpour that made the windowpanes look like lead as the rain beat against them. Lonnie lighted a lamp and sat down in the rocking chair beside the stove. He hated the glare of the bulb that hung from the ceiling, preferring the old kerosene lamp instead. It did give a softer, prettier light, but the night was so dreary that any light, glaring or soft, mattered little in the face of our gloomy mood.

Janey snapped on her radio which she had lately left with me so that I might enjoy it while I was alone during the day. A band was playing, and some rather silly female voice was singing something about life being a bowl of cherries. Janey stood listening for a minute; then, wrinkling her nose at the unseen singer, she hastily switched to another station. We leaned back in our chairs, not much interested in the radio until a phrase caught our attention. A man was talking, and he had just mentioned "the wild children of the road." It seemed to be a program of editorial comment. I was interested right away.

"They are a growing army," he said. "There are hundreds of them on the roads this winter; most of them are boys in their teens. There are a few girls too, not many—about one in twenty. Then there are scores of younger children, some of them so very young that one marvels at their survival. They come from all over the country, this children's army. They come from the cities where the unemployment of a father often means too little food for too many mouths. They come from the farms where the incredibly low prices of produce have been as tragic for the farm family. They don't know where they're going or why. They simply move on—on to the next door for a

184

handout or maybe a curse, on to the next packing box or sand cave for a bed.

"They hop freights, and in so doing dozens of them are killed or crippled. They hitchhike; they beg and steal and fight one another. They are half-starved, scantily dressed, susceptible to diseases brought on by malnutrition and exposure. They ought to be in warm and comfortable homes; they ought to be in school. Instead, they are struggling through an icy winter, lucky if they are able to stay alive from one day to another.

"Here in Omaha this afternoon police were summoned to a dilapidated barn just outside the city limits where the high winds that accompanied today's severe rainstorm caused a wall to collapse, pinning a fourteen-year-old youth under a heavy oak beam. The boy was hospitalized as soon as he was removed from the wreckage; doctors say his condition is critical. Of the other eight children who had spent the last three days in the barn, five were found to be suffering from varying degrees of malnutrition. Two of them are twelve-year-old cousins who say their home is in Des Moines, Iowa; another is a ten-year-old boy from Chicago who looked, as one newsman put it, like a half-famished angel with a shock of blond hair and an old banjo which he clutched in lieu of a harp—"

I don't think that I made a sound, but I felt a

scream inside me. Lonnie said, "My God, my God, it's Joey. It has to be Joey."

Dimly after a minute I began to hear the words from the radio again. " ... aroused the compassion of many citizens of Omaha who tonight have opened their homes to these desperately needy children. A few of the wild boys of the road are in good hands tonight. But they are only a few. Hundreds of others are out in the fields, on the highways, in the poorer sections of towns and cities. They are raiding garbage cans; they are burning anything they can find in an effort to keep warm. Not since the Crusades have so many children suffered so cruelly. And this is the United States of America in the year of our Lord, 1933."

Lonnie was pulling on his coat. "I'll go to the radio station. See what they know. They can surely tell me what people to contact next. I'll find him. I'll find that boy if it takes all night—all week—"

"Let me go with you, Lonnie," I begged.

"Don't be a fool, Josh." His voice was harsh. "Do you think I want *you* going into a relapse when we don't know what to expect about Joey? You stay right here. I've got enough to worry about."

He hurried outside, and through the din made by the rain we heard the sound of his old car as it sputtered into action. Janey put her hand on my arm. "He's all worked up, Josh. He was like this the night we found you. He almost took my head off when I asked him a few questions about you that night."

I sat down, suddenly very tired. "We're causing him trouble and expense—we're making him worry. I hate to think about it," I said.

She sat down beside me on the bench behind the stove, and we clasped hands; somehow it seemed the natural thing to do. The room was shadowy in the lamplight.

"Do you want me to talk or be quiet?" Janey asked.

"Be quiet," I answered.

"Do you want me to stay here or go over home and leave you alone?"

"I want you to stay here—I want you very much, Janey. Just stay here like this."

She nodded, and we sat there for a long time, close to one another without moving. Gramma came over later to iron the shirts in a big laundry basket which Lonnie had carried in for her earlier, the work that gave her a chance to earn a little money to help with expenses. I thought Gramma might not like it that Janey and I were sitting together with our hands clasped, but she seemed to feel it was all right. She said to Janey, "It's like when we had our Davy with us. You'd sit there behind the stove holding each other by the hand—you remember?"

Janey nodded and smiled at the deaf old woman; then she turned to me. "She's right, you

187

know. Davy and I used to sit like this. Especially if one or both of us had been scolded. We'd just sit here holding each other's hand and staring in front of us. Lonnie and Aunt Helen used to say it was unnerving. I think, unconsciously, we meant it to be that way."

"You liked him a lot, didn't you?"

"I adored him. He was just enough older to make me feel that whatever he did was right. Anything, of course, that didn't interfere with me. We fought once in a while. Not often, but when we did, it was a bloody fight."

We didn't say anything more. I watched Gramma take a hot flatiron from the stove and push it slowly back and forth along a white shirt sleeve, making little inroads at the top of the cuff, pressing slowly and heavily across the cuff itself. The rain continued to beat against the windows, stubbornly persisting, I thought, long after you'd think there couldn't be any more water to come down. It seemed Lonnie had been gone an age; I wondered what could have happened. I wondered if it could have been a mistake, if by some cruel chance there could have been another boy from Chicago who was clutching an old banjo.

We waited hour after hour. At nine Janey remembered that we hadn't had supper, and so she filled bowls with soup and the three of us ate a little. At ten she and Gramma hung the long rows of shirts, each on its separate hanger, in Lonnie's bedroom, ready to be packed and delivered the next day. Then Gramma drew a shawl around her shoulders and motioned to Janey. "We must go, honey. It may be late before Uncle Lonnie gets home. You have to get to bed." She came over and, to my surprise, bent and kissed my forehead. "My prayers have been for your little brother ever since you came, Josh; tonight they will be the same," she said. It was strange that I had ever thought of her as being grim.

When they were gone, I walked around the room a dozen times or more, stopping at the window to look out into the night, going back to the bench where Janey and I had sat together. After a while I began to tremble; I didn't think it was with cold, but I put more coal on the fire anyway and drew a blanket around my shoulders. "I mustn't get sick again," I thought. "Lonnie has had enough trouble in taking care of me; I've got to take some responsibility for myself. I've got to keep well and take care of Joey——"

A car turned into the driveway finally and stopped as near the kitchen door as the driver could maneuver it. I stood at the window, shaking, trying to see out into the darkness. I found myself saying, "Please—please—," through my chattering teeth.

Then I heard Lonnie at the door, and I threw it open for him. He came inside, carrying Joey in his arms. "I have a young man here who says he's acquainted with you, Josh." Lonnie's voice was cheerful, consciously so, I realized. He put Joey

189

down in the big armchair and drew aside a layer of blankets, revealing a terribly thin little boy, dressed in warm, clean pajamas, his feet tucked in wooly, white slippers. He didn't quite look like Joey except for the big gray eyes and the mass of blond hair that fell around his face.

There are patterns of behavior that people of a certain age, a certain sex, a certain condition, must follow. A fifteen-year-old boy cannot take a ten-year-old brother in his arms as a mother might do; he cannot say the things that are deep inside him, cannot express his love and relief, his bitter remorse. The pattern of behavior toward a younger brother by a fifteen-year-old does not allow these things. Joey would have recognized this. He understood patterns very well.

And I so I simply held out my hand. "Hi, Joey," I said.

He grinned every so slightly. That grin belonged to the Joey of other days. He said, "Hi, Josh. It's sure good to see you."

We shook hands. I ducked my head a little so that he wouldn't know that I was crying. Tears were not in the pattern either.

Chapter Ten

We put Joey to bed, and when I leaned over him, he gave a long sigh of contentment and looked up at me. Then he went to sleep almost immediately. I sat close to the bed and watched him as he slept. It took me a little while to realize fully that he was there, that the long nightmare of anxiety and anguish was over. Lonnie dropped down in a chair facing me, and for a time he just sat there staring ahead of him as if he, too, were emerging from some bad dream.

"It's been a night," he said finally, leaning his head against the back of the chair and closing his eyes.

"Did you have trouble finding him, Lonnie?"

"Not in finding him. The police had a list of the

people who had taken the eight children this afternoon. Joey was with a couple who appear to be in good circumstances, and they didn't want to give him up. He was clean and fed and dressed in warm night clothes; they'd sent for a doctor; they'd done everything they could and so resented me at first. The woman, Mrs. Arthur, cried and took on over him; at first I thought maybe they were right, maybe I had no business moving him while he's so frail. But Joey is the one who settled things. He intended coming home with me and finding his brother—there were no if's about it. He was weak, but he raised Cain when he thought I was going to leave without him."

I went over to the stove and poured a cup of coffee for him. He nodded his thanks. "The doctor came and examined him. He said it was better for me to bring him home if he was going to fret. I couldn't help but feel sorry for the Arthurs. They'd only had him a few hours, but they were in love with him already." Lonnie sipped his coffee slowly. "Lord, this is good. They offered me food over there, but I couldn't eat. I was all shook to pieces."

I looked at the little hand that lay outside the blanket. "Do you think he'll be all right, Lonnie?"

"Oh, yes. The doctor says it's just a matter of food and rest—and love—for Joey. We shouldn't feed him much at a time, but he must have something every few hours. You and Janey will have to

No Promises in the Wind

watch over him for a few days. He'll be all right.
The doctor thinks so too."

"I wish the folks knew," I said more to myself
than to Lonnie.

"They do," he said. "I went out while they were
getting Joey ready to come home, and sent a wire
to your folks and one to Pete Harris. I just said,
'Found Joey. Everything's okay.' I hope your dad
can sleep tonight."

"I hope so too," I said. A kind of gladness for
Dad went through my mind.

When he had finished his coffee, Lonnie stood
up and began unbuttoning his shirt. "I think I'll
have to get to bed if I'm to work tomorrow, Josh.
I'm beat. Can you watch over him tonight?"

"Of course." I looked up at him. In the space of
a few months he had helped us to a chance to
take care of ourselves, and when we had failed at
that, he had saved both our lives. I said, "You
took a big load on your shoulders that day you
stopped your truck and waited for us, Lonnie."

He smiled just a little. "No regrets. Good-night,
Josh." He turned the lamp down low, closing the
door behind him.

For the first time in what seemed like an eternity, I was once again alone with Joey. I couldn't
bear to go to bed; I had to sit there in the dim
light and look at Joey while he slept. Somehow I
was afraid to go to sleep; I had to stay awake and
be sure that the miracle of finding him was real.

He woke up after an hour or so, and I heated

some milk and brought it to him. I sat on the bed at his back so he could lean against me when he sat up. He drank the milk eagerly and when he was through, lifted his hand and reached for mine.

"I found you, didn't I?" he said.

I held his hand tightly in mine. It was a terribly thin little hand, so thin that it made a shudder run over me when I realized the narrow margin by which I had been allowed to have him with me again. I said, "Can you tell me what happened, Joey? Just a little before you go back to sleep?"

"Yes." He hesitated, and his face showed the pain of remembering that night when we quarreled. "I went back to the shed," he said finally. "I stayed there all night, and I waited and waited the next day. I thought sure you'd come back, but when you didn't, I thought I'd better try to get home."

He was silent for a long time. "If it tires you, Joey, don't talk. You can tell me tomorrow."

"No. I'm just trying to get words to tell you. I started to hitchhike home, but I had such a feeling that I was doing the wrong thing. I kept thinking you needed me. So I came back to Omaha. I thought you'd be here."

"Why didn't you call Lonnie when you got there, Joey?"

"It was awful. I couldn't remember his last name. I think we mentioned it just once down at the carnival. I tried and tried to remember, but I
194

couldn't. I was just lost in Omaha—looking for a man named Lonnie."

I couldn't talk much. "You mustn't get tired," I told him. "Better go to sleep now."

He shook his head. "I've got to tell you one thing, Josh. I didn't know that you were sick with fever that night. Lonnie told me as we were coming home. He told me you were so sick and scared you didn't know what you were doing."

"There's never any real excuse for being as mean as I was, Joey. But it's true that I *was* awfully sick and scared."

"I know you were. Like Dad, I guess, the night he turned on you."

He burrowed down under the covers and was asleep almost as soon as the words were spoken. But I sat there staring straight ahead into the shadows for a long time.

The picture was painful, but there it was, clear and sharp before me. Suddenly, for the first time that winter I wanted to go home. Without warning, a wave of such homesickness as I'd never felt before came over me. I could think of nothing but Dad, of sleepless nights for him like the ones I had known, of remorse and anguish as bitter for him as mine had been for me. I had remembered the black looks and the mean, cruel words all winter, remembering them in great detail to help maintain the dislike for him which I'd thought would never change. But at Joey's words there in the darkness, I felt only pity and a sense of hav-

195

No Promises in the Wind

ing been subjected to the same hell Dad had
known. I hoped I wouldn't undergo a change of
feeling the next morning; I felt better and more
mature; I felt a compassion that was altogether
new to me.

I tried being matter-of-fact with myself. No
point in kidding myself that Dad and I would ever
be able to live together without running into
problems. We were too much alike. I remembered
times when he had apologized to Mom for a show
of impatience toward her on his part. "It's the
Grondowski in me, Mary," he would tell her, blaming the father he resented for his own weaknesses. I had often tended to write off my own
weaknesses as being inherited from Dad. It occurred to me as I lay there beside Joey in the
silent room that both Stefan and Josh Grondowski should stop blaming their fathers and work on
a little self-discipline and understanding themselves. I wondered if someday I might talk to Dad
about the weaknesses we shared.

I couldn't settle down to sleep; the thoughts
kept whirling around in my head. It seemed in-
credible to me that the wish to go home should
all at once be so strong inside me. How easy it
would have been to catch rides back to Chicago
when we were healthy; now Joey would not be
strong for many weeks, and my cough was still
with me, my legs too weak for more than walking
around the rooms of Lonnie's house. Besides that,
there was a great debt which we owed Lonnie.

Somehow I had to get well and find a job so that I could repay him before we left. That was a matter of great importance to me. One thing to Stefan Grondowski's credit was the fact that he had taught his sons to be honest about their debts; that much I believed I would have admitted even when my anger against him was bitterest.

The prospect of repaying a debt, however, was very dim. We were penniless, neither of us well enough to take care of ourselves. "If I can get rid of this cough and gain some strength, maybe Lonnie can find work for me here in Omaha. Or maybe I can take Joey back to Chicago and then set out for the carnival when Pete gets it going again. Maybe with summer coming on . . ." The maybes cluttered up my brain and made my temples throb.

At two o'clock Joey awoke and I fed him some soup that had kept warm on the back of the stove; at six I was up making a hot cereal for him, but Gramma came over and made me go back to bed while she finished the cooking and, with many little murmurs of sympathy, gave Joey his breakfast.

Joey began to recuperate immediately. With each meal we could see new brightness come into his face, new light in his eyes. Janey became his special nurse, and I sometimes caught a twinkle in my young brother's eyes, a twinkle that seemed to crow over me as Janey hovered above him, feeding him, reading to him, pampering him as much as he would allow.

Mrs. Arthur, the woman who with her husband had taken Joey into their home the night Lonnie found him, came to visit him on his third day with us. She was an attractive woman, nicely dressed and smelling faintly of a perfume that was like spring flowers. She exclaimed over Joey and cried a little as she sat beside him. Finally she turned to speak to me as I stood at the head of his bed.

"You are the brother he was looking for—you are Josh?" she asked.

"Yes."

"I could have kept Joey for a while—I could have had the joy of nursing him back to health if he hadn't been so anxious to see his brother." She looked at me almost resentfully although she smiled.

"We're very grateful to you, ma'am. I can't ever thank you enough for what you did for Joey that night."

Her face relaxed somewhat. "Mr. Bromer told us a great deal of what you boys have lived through this winter. He mentioned that you play the piano quite well."

"I—I enjoy playing," I answered.

"How long have you studied?"

"My mother gave me lessons until a couple years ago when we had to sell our piano. Since then I've learned on my own."

"Oh," she said, and looked down at her gloved hands as if she took little stock in the kind of lessons one learns from his own mother.

Then Joey spoke up. "If you'd hear my brother play, you'd understand, Mrs. Arthur. He's really top-notch."

She smiled down at him. "Then I'd like to hear him play, Joey; maybe when you're well, you and your brother and Mr. Bromer's niece can come to my house and we'll hear Josh play. Would you like that?"

He nodded, delighted. I didn't feel so enthusiastic myself. I had a feeling that she was a woman who would have suffered if music familiar to her was subjected to a little improvisation, a beat that was a little different. But I thanked her. "Yes, I'd like to play for you," I said, but I didn't think it likely that I ever would.

She left books and games for Joey, some special things to eat and some articles of clothing which she said had once belonged to her own children, but which looked suspiciously new. She also brought his old jacket, the twenty dollar overshoes, and the knife with Pete Harris's initials in the handle. And, carefully wrapped as if she knew it was precious, was Howie's banjo in a large cardboard box.

During the next few days when Joey and I were alone, I got out pen and paper and began the letters I needed to write. I wrote home first of all. In the beginning I wrote, "Dear Mom"; then after a long time I added, "and Dad." I told them how Joey had been found, how fast he was recuperating, how comfortable and safe we were with Lonnie. I didn't say that I'd been homesick, that I wanted to bring Joey home soon. I couldn't quite say that, but I felt that my letter would certainly reassure them. I told them a little about Janey; I sent our love to Kitty.

After that I wrote to Edward C., and then to Emily. I didn't know whether she was Mrs. Pete Harris or not; I simply directed the letter to "Emily in care of Pete Harris." She had asked me to write to her, and I had wondered what I would ever have to say to her, and I had wondered what I would ever have to say to her. I found that it wasn't hard. I used up page after page in telling her the whole story—in sharing my anxiety and then my joy with her.

We were a happy family during those last weeks of March, so happy that I almost forgot the loneliness for home which I had felt earlier. The attention of all of us was centered upon Joey, and our common concern over him made us a tightly drawn little group. Lonnie was especially cheerful these days. He would come home bring ing treats for supper—oysters because they were Gramma's favorite food, ice cream because that was Joey's. One night when I had lost all traces of my cough, he took Janey and me to a movie, leaving Gramma and Joey at home with a big bowl of popcorn he had fixed for them.

He spoke of us as his three kids. He would ask Janey to read aloud in the evening, and we would sit around the table listening, Lonnie on the old couch, resting his arm around Joey's shoulders. I noticed Gramma watching him on one such night as she stood at her ironing board. There were tears in her eyes.

As I grew stronger, I began to think more and more about getting a job. The bread of charity choked me a little now and then; I felt that the proudest moment of my life would come when I could begin to repay Lonnie for what he'd done for us. And when all was repaid—then, perhaps, home. Perhaps. I wasn't quite sure, but I thought that home was what I wanted.

Lonnie recognized my restlessness and need for work. "Sure, sure, Josh. I'll keep my eyes open; something might turn up. We've got to be careful, though. You've lost twenty pounds this winter. I can't let you take on too much until you're husky again."

And then one evening Mrs. Arthur appeared again. She asked Lonnie if she might pick the three of us up and take us to her house for lunch the next day.

Lonnie smiled at her. "Are you sure you want Josh and Janey, or just this lady-killer here?" he asked, indicating Joey.

She was a pleasant woman, ready to laugh. She said, "Joey is my first love, yes, but I want the others too. I want to hear Josh play just to see if what his little brother says about him is true."

Lonnie loaned me a decent shirt, and I carefully pressed the old trousers Pete Harris had given me. Joey was fairly well supplied with the clothing Mrs. Arthur had brought him earlier. Janey, of course, had no problems. She wore her best blue cotton dress and tied her hair back with a band of blue velvet. Her costume brought praise from the three male members of her family, a praise that deepened the color in her cheeks, overcoming the freckles and making her very pretty.

Mrs. Arthur picked us up at eleven o'clock. She had a friendly way about her that put us at ease as we drove along and stopped finally at a house in a neighborhood obviously much wealthier than the one in which Lonnie lived.

The Arthur home seemed magnificent to us, but the great piano in an alcove off the living room was the one point of interest as far as I was concerned. I walked toward it, forgetting the other three, unaware at first that they stood watching me, smiling at my fascination with the beautiful instrument.

"We will leave you and the piano alone for a while, Josh," Mrs. Arthur said, coming over to my side. "You may want to get your hands accustomed to the keyboard again before you play for me. Go ahead. It's all yours for the next hour before we eat."

It was the finest instrument I had ever touched, and the beautiful resonant tones that responded to my fingers thrilled me so much that I forgot everything except my own delight. I roamed the keyboard for a time, softly at first and then with mounting excitement.

I had improvised upon a love theme for Emily down on the carnival grounds, but as I sat at Mrs. Arthur's piano, my improvisations covered a wider scope. It was as if a long story passed before my eyes and became music somewhere inside my brain. I forgot where I was, forgot that someone might be listening, and I played as I watched Howie's body carried down a long track; I played as I remembered a boy standing humiliated before a pretty girl who told him she was sorry he must beg; I played as I relived the fear of cold and hunger, the anguish of losing Joey, and finally the surge of gratitude that the world had righted itself for me, had restored my confidence.

When I was through, I realized that Mrs. Arthur and Janey and Joey were standing near me. Janey's eyes were large and grave when I looked up at her.

"I don't know you, Josh," she said just above a whisper.

Mrs. Arthur stood there looking at me. I couldn't tell what she was thinking. Finally she said, "You were improvising, weren't you?"

"Yes," I said. I thought she probably didn't like it.

"And you've only had lessons with your mother?"

"Yes. She's a fine teacher, though."

"I believe you, Josh." She looked at me thoughtfully. "You'd like a job playing somewhere, wouldn't you?"

"I don't think you can imagine how much I want a job like that."

"Well"—she looked down at Joey's face which was full of pride for me—"we'll have to see, Joey. We'll have to see if we can't find a job of some sort for your brother."

I don't remember much about the lunch. It was delicious, whatever it was, and served on thin china that Janey could later describe to Gramma in detail. Mrs. Arthur was gay and pleasant; Joey and Janey were at ease and chatted with her all during the meal. I alone was silent. It seemed as if I were in a dream, and I only came out of it when the others teased me. Mrs. Arthur smiled at me. "It's a promise, Josh. I'll find someone who will pay for music like yours."

That day marked the point when the dream Howie and I had shared began to take form. Within a week Mrs. Arthur came over to see me.

"I've talked to a lot of people, Josh. Last night my husband and I talked to the manager of a very fine restaurant here. The manager, Mr. Ericsson, is a friend of my husband's. We persuaded him it would be a good idea to feature music from six until midnight, creating a job for a boy and

204

No Promises in the Wind

doing a good thing for himself too. I told him quite a lot about you—how much I liked your music—and since he respects my knowledge of music, he wants to hear you play tomorrow afternoon. I'll drive you over."

It was as if a long nightmare had given way to a fairy tale. Mr. Ericsson liked my playing. The salary, in comparison to the five dollars a week which I had received at the carnival, seemed princely to me. Mrs. Arthur took me to a shop and fitted me with an appropriate suit and shoes; she wanted to give them to me, but I jotted down the costs and prepared to repay her as soon as I had money. Begging had left its scars, scars that hurt again even at the kindliest of gifts.

My work at the restaurant gave me a great deal of satisfaction. There was no silly clowning to be carried out as had been necessary to the job down at the carnival. I was a well-dressed, poised young man who played as I wanted to play, who responded courteously to requests.

One point bothered me at first, but, of necessity, I quickly pushed it to the back of my mind. Mr. Ericsson had placed a printed page titled "Our Wild Boy of the Road" inside the menu covers. There the diners could read about Joey and me, about the fact that we left home because our family didn't have enough to eat. There was a detailed account of the begging, of the freezing and starving we had endured. It shamed me at first. Our troubles were a drawing card like poor

205

Ellsworth's flippers that had grown instead of arms, like Madame Olympia's mountain of flesh, like Edward C. Kensington's dwarfism and the pitiful hump on his back. But it was not a time for sensitivity. A job was so precious a thing, so much a gift right out of Heaven, that I had no right to protest. I didn't tell Joey about it, though, nor Janey. But one night I told Lonnie. His lips tightened, and his eyes looked angry for a moment. But he didn't say anything.

It wasn't long until Mr. Ericsson decided to feature Joey with me. There had been an account in the papers as well as on the radio of the boy who looked like "a half-famished angel" clasping a banjo in lieu of a harp. People wanted to see the younger "wild boy." And so, after I had worked with him for hours, helping him to accompany me when I played some old or popular ballads, Joey stood beside me on the platform, singing and playing ringing chords on Howie's old banjo.

He was a great attraction; his fragile appearance and beauty as well as a natural gift for comedy made him an immediate hit. Diners didn't care if he stumbled over the chords occasionally. There would be a little flurry of laughter when his voice suddenly wandered off-key; then when he grinned widely and got himself straightened out with some help from me, he'd receive a burst of laughing applause.

Joey accepted his success as casually as he accepted the fact that most people loved him at first sight. It was just a fact of life to him; nothing to get excited about. But to me, our success was so marvelous a thing that I couldn't get used to it. Several times I woke up in the night and for a second I thought that I was somewhere out in the fields or in the train depot of some lonely little town and that I'd had a dream of something too wonderful to be true. The wonder eased that loneliness I'd felt for home the night of Joey's return. Home kept receding from my mind as the nights passed, gay, pleasant nights when I played for well-dressed, happy people who could afford to dine in beautiful restaurants. And then at the end of the week there was a check—money to pay our debts, money to make us feel confident and secure.

We sent money home from time to time, and we gave almost all the rest of it to Lonnie. He accepted it without comment, but I had the feeling he was not using it to help with household expenses.

"We owe you this money, Lonnie. It's yours. We don't want to be leeches on you."

Lonnie was almost curt with me. "People don't want to be paid for some things. Sure, I'll keep a little money for medicines and extra expenses. I do that because I like the way you boys fight to keep your self-respect in money matters. But don't ask me to take money for the food you've eaten or the bed you've slept in. You know about my boy; you must know how I feel about you and

Joey." He folded and refolded the bills I'd given him. "You boys will need this when you go back to Chicago," he added.

I didn't like for him to mention going back to Chicago. It brought a strangely mixed feeling of homesickness, of guilt and resentment that Joey and I should be asked to give up something better than our best hopes and go back to something once bitter and still unsure.

The mail brought word from Emily one day, an envelope addressed in a high, delicate script that looked as if every letter had been drawn painstakingly. The writing looked like Emily, I thought, and I opened the envelope carefully so that no part of my name as she had written it would be destroyed.

She told me of the relief and joy of Pete, of Edwad C., of her boys and herself, when they heard that Joey was safe and that I was recovering from pneumonia. She said, "We had you boys with us for only a few weeks, but you made your way into our affections. We will never forget you, never stop wishing the very best of good fortune for both of you."

She sent messages from Pete and Edward C; she told me a little of how Pete was rebuilding his carnival which he would bring farther north in the summer. There was only one mention of her marriage: "My boys are happy to have a father once again, and Pete is a kind and understanding father." That was all. I wondered if she were happy too. I hoped so.

Then, like Lonnie, she talked about my going home. "I beg you, Josh, to take your little brother home, to make peace with your father and to gladden your mother's heart. Parents are sometimes very wrong—I know that well enough. But unless they are really evil, they agonize over their mistakes. Your parents are not evil, Josh; they couldn't have produced two beautiful boys like you and Joey if they were. I beg you again—please go home."

I played at the restaurant six nights a week, and because I had to practice many hours of the day, I had very little opportunity to see Janey. But on my one night off we'd take long walks, talking of one thing and another, sometimes coming home to sit together with our hands clasped as she and Lonnie's boy used to do.

Spring was late that year, but week by week the days grew warmer, the air gentler. One evening as Janey and I walked together a misty rain enveloped us, hardly enough to make us bother with an umbrella, but enough to make little wisps of her hair curl against Janey's cheeks, to make her skin glow with the tiny drops of mist that moistened it.

"You are my girl, aren't you, Janey?" I asked her.

"Yes," she said, "I've been your girl ever since

that afternoon you told me that I didn't need to wear earrings like Emily—"

"—and you pressed your cheek against my hand. I've loved you ever since then, Janey—I always will, as long as I live."

She didn't answer for a while. Then she stopped and faced me as we reached a little clump of trees in the park. "Lonnie has talked to me, Josh. He thinks that you and Joey should go home to your mother and dad. He told me that I mustn't try to keep you here because I—I—care so much for you. And I won't. I'll be terribly lonely when you and Joey are gone—but we must listen to Lonnie. He's always known what was best for me. He knew what was best for you when you were down and out; he must know what is best now that things are better."

She was right and I knew it, but all kinds of feelings churned inside me as I thought about leaving her. "I don't know what to do, Janey. I'm pulled in all directions—I can't quite figure out what is right."

She lifted her arms then and placed her hands on my shoulders. I drew her to me. "I'll come back to you, Janey," I whispered. "I'll come back. You'll see. Just as soon as I make things right with my parents, I'll come back."

She said, "Yes, of course, Josh. At least I hope so." I could see that she didn't quite accept my promise. Janey had lost her parents, a cousin she adored, an aunt who had been almost like a second mother to her. She didn't really believe that the people she loved ever came back.

The next days were full of inner turmoil and uncertainty for me. My love for Janey was very real and tender; I knew, though, that we were very young, and that a thing called marriage which people in love always thought about was something so far in the future as to be unreal. But that made our love no less true. I wanted to strike out at anyone who dared to say we were too young to understand love.

Lonnie came and stood beside me one evening as I stood staring at nothing from the window. He was silent as if waiting for me to speak.

"You know that Janey and I love one another, don't you?"

"Yes, I know," he answered.

"Don't call it puppy love, Lonnie."

"No, I'm not one to downgrade love—at any age. What I wanted to say to you is this: Your going home is not the most final thing in the world. You've been successful on a job out here; you've made friends who will help you to find a job if you don't find one in Chicago. And as for Janey—this feeling between you and her *could* last as long as you live. It *could* change too— you've got to face that. But let's suppose it lasts. You'll always be welcome in my home—even if you only come to see Janey."

He smiled at me, and I felt comforted. My bitter winter had ended in good fortune. It gave me hope for the years ahead. That night I played for the diners at Mr. Ericsson's restaurant with a lighter heart, with a greater feeling of optimism.

Mr. Ericsson asked me to help Joey increase his repertoire of appealing songs, and in thinking about the list which we might choose from, I remembered Dad's old Polish song, *Góalru, Czy Ci Nie Zal?,** which was the one that came back to me on the awful night when I believed I was going to die. I think that as a little boy I had been impressed by the expression on Dad's face when he taught me the words. "It is a song about the yearning for home," he had told me, and I had interpreted that as meaning a yearning for his native country. Now, I knew that it might be a yearning for the mountains of Poland or the beaches of Spain or the dreariness of Chicago's west side.

For several mornings Joey and I rehearsed together while the restaurant was still closed. I taught him the Polish words, and he learned to accompany me softly and with tenderness on Howie's banjo.

"It's beautiful, isn't it, Josh?" he said.

"I think so. I've loved it since I was a little boy."

Joey took a deep breath. "It hurts me, though. It makes me want to see Mom and Dad." He ran his fingers over the strings of the banjo. The chords sounded lonely, just as they had sounded

* See page 224.

that night on the freight train when Howie had strummed his banjo for a minute and then laid it aside.

"You want to go home, don't you, Joey?" I asked after a minute.

He nodded without looking up at me. "If you do," he said.

"All right, we'll go home. Everyone advises it— all the people who care about us. I think perhaps they're right. It's time we headed for home."

I talked to Mr. Ericsson that afternoon. I told him how we felt, what we had to do. He was a kind man. He gave me a letter of recommendation and suggested places in Chicago where I might present it. We shook hands, and I hoped I had made him realize how much I appreciated what he'd done for us.

The Arthurs invited Lonnie and Janey and Gramma to have dinner with them that night at the restaurant. When the audience asked Joey and me for an encore, I looked down into their faces and did what I had never done before: I made an announcement. "Joey and I will sing you a Polish song tonight, a song that tells about a longing for home. You people here in Omaha have been kind to us; we'll never forget you. But now we have to go. The 'Wild Boys of the Road' have been gone a long time, and tonight they're homesick."

Then Joey and I sang Dad's song, and people applauded us as they never had before.

Chapter Eleven

Although we had already told the Arthurs good-bye, Mrs. Arthur wanted to see Joey again before we left. So Lonnie took him over that last evening, giving Janey and me a chance to talk together out on the back steps while Gramma busied herself inside the kitchen. The stars were thick in the sky that night, and the air was warm and fragrant. The icy winter of Nebraska was far away, its violence something hard to remember.

Our thoughts were all about the fact that we would soon be parted. "It isn't so far, you know. I can take a train in Chicago and be back in a few hours," I said.

"Yes, I know." Janey bent forward, elbows on her knees, chin in her cupped hands.

"You want me to come back, don't you, Janey?"

"I sure do."

"And—and I hope you won't forget me. Of course, as Lonnie says, if other boys ask you to go out with them, naturally you should go—"

"Oh, I will," she said, too readily I thought.

"Sometimes I wonder, Janey . . ."

I felt her little shoulder grow tense as it leaned against me. She swallowed hard before she spoke. "Look, Josh, you could make me cry—awful easy. But I'm not going to do it. I dread to see you leave. This place is going to be haunted by you because I—I—*think* I love you, but—"

I was suddenly edgy and irritated. "You just *think* so. Aren't you sure, Janey?"

"Were *you* sure when you loved that Emily lady?"

I took her hand and held it in both of mine while I thought about what she had said. "That was not the same," I finally told her.

"No? And maybe it won't be the same as this when you find some girl who doesn't have freckles and—and isn't a nut—and looks good in earrings."

"Lonnie's been talking to you," I said.

"He has not. I wouldn't let him. I've thought these things out for myself because I know things that you and Lonnie don't understand. I happen to be a woman and I—"

I laughed at her. "You're only fourteen, Janey."

She choked suddenly and hid her face in her hands. "I'm not as sure as I sound, Josh. I—I don't know what it's all about. I wish I could be sure, but I can't. Not *really* sure."

We sat together for a long time, each of us thinking our own thoughts. When Lonnie and Joey came home, we didn't have much to say to them either. And at nine when Janey had to go home, I kissed her good-night right in front of Lonnie. I didn't care.

We left for the train to Chicago a little before daylight the next morning. We said good-bye to Gramma before we left the house; then Joey climbed into the front seat of the car with Lonnie while Janey and I sat together in the back. We were all silent, and I think the others were as heavy-hearted as I was.

Joey and I had tickets for the homeward trip. We had a right to step inside the coach in full view of any train official who chanced to be near; we could sit on the comfortable green mohair seats and have the privilege of feeling the miles slide by without blisters or weariness or pain on our part. Physical pain, that is, for the sight and sounds of a train still sent a shiver of horror through us. But we knew that it was a horror we must overcome. I saw Joey set his shoulders and try to repress the shudder that shook him when he looked at the big wheels of the engine.

No Promises in the Wind

We stood around feeling stiff and unnatural, dreading the good-byes, wishing they were over. Lonnie said, "Maybe it's just as well you board a little early and get settled," so we moved down the platform to our coach. There Joey said good-bye to Janey, and we tried to thank Lonnie but he wouldn't have it. "Look, you fellows, write to us—write often, and don't forget us," he said. He looked at me with his half-smile. "You stay and say good-bye to Janey. Joey and I will get on and find a place for your baggage."

Janey and I stood in the near-darkness together for several minutes. I guess we said the things that most people say when they love one another and a train is waiting to separate them for months, maybe for years, maybe for all time. I hoped she wouldn't cry, and she didn't. Finally I whispered, "Good-bye, Janey," and I left her quickly.

Then, at last, Joey and I were in our seats, and after a few minutes the train pulled out slowly as we waved our good-byes from the window. Neither of us said anything for quite a long time after that.

Daylight opened up over the prairies within an hour, and we watched the play of colors as they appeared before us from growing crops, from freshly plowed soil, from woods and streams and blue skies. There wasn't a trace of the ice or cold or howling blizzards we had known in that country during the winter, but now and then we saw a tired-looking figure plodding along that may have been a boy my age hunting the next town to ask for work or a handout. At one spot a group of men waved a coffeepot at us as they stood beside a fire they had built near the tracks. Sometimes when we stopped at a station we saw placards reading, "As Right as Roosevelt." One of them had been defaced by lines that seemed to slash the words angrily; on another someone had written, "Yes, God bless him."

We passed a freight occasionally as our passenger train sped down the track. Often there were men standing at the open doors of boxcars, men sitting on top of cars, their legs dangling over the edge. They might have been the same hopeless-looking men who traveled west with us the night we left Chicago—the hobo who helped Joey into the car, or the one who gave us a can of beans when we got off somewhere in Nebraska.

Once when we stopped at a station we saw a white-coated boy carrying sandwiches and milk and coffee toward the train. "Would you like something to eat?" I asked, and Joey said, "Yes, I'm starving."

The words were no sooner out than he looked at me aghast. "What a dumb thing to say," he muttered.

It wasn't dumb, but it *was* strange; he had never once said that when he was, in truth, starving.

We ate slowly and comfortably. The coach was

not full, and so we removed our shoes and stretched our stockinged feet to the seat opposite us. Joey scooted down a little in his seat so that he could make his toes extend as far forward as mine. "You've grown, Joey," I said to him. "In spite of all the things that would stunt most kids, you've been determined to grow."

He smiled with the satisfaction he'd always shown at any praise of mine. The conductor came along and pretended to snip Joey's nose with the ticket punch he carried. "You boys been on a vacation?" he asked.

We looked at one another. "Well, in a way," I said. The conductor really wasn't much interested; he nodded and walked on.

A woman stopped him a few seats forward, and we heard his answer to her question. "We should be getting into Chicago in just about two hours, ma'am," he said. I felt a shudder inside me at his words.

I wondered if our folks would seem like strangers, if we'd have to get acquainted again, if home would seem a lonely place where we'd be homesick for Lonnie and Gramma and Janey. Mom would be happy to see us, I could be sure of that. And I could talk to her. I could tell her about playing at the carnival and at the restaurant in Omaha. I could tell her about Janey, and sometime I might just possibly tell her about Emily. And as for Kitty, she'd be interested in everything—I could depend on Kitty. I wondered if I should go to see Howie's mother, wondered if she'd really care if she heard about what had happened to Howie. I thought I would go and see Miss Crowne, would show her the letter of recommendation Mr. Ericsson had given me. Maybe she'd know of a part-time job.

Finally I had to face what I dreaded. There would be Dad. What would he be like, I wondered. What would we say to one another? I thought about the memory I'd had of him, the memory of him rocking me in front of the fire. I decided I'd tell him about that. Maybe it would help us if he knew that when things were blackest, I had remembered a time when we were close to one another.

I felt worried and restless. "I don't know, Joey; I don't know just how we're going to get along in Chicago. We've had a taste of good luck, but times are still bad."

Joey wasn't worried. "After all we've been through, I guess we can handle Chicago," he said indifferently as he leaned his head against the back of his seat.

I couldn't allow the young cock-of-the-walk to see too much of my fear. "I guess so," I said, and managed to smile a little.

Soon the shabby old neighborhoods that bordered the railroad tracks began to appear, tired-looking and decrepit even in the summer sunlight. Buildings huddled together closely, and the smokestacks of factories stood like laborers' bare arms lifted to the sky; smoke curled from some of them, but others looked cold and dead. The train began to move more slowly, and people all around us bustled about to collect their baggage from the racks above the seats. "We won't reach the station for a half hour or so," the conductor told someone, but people didn't care. They wanted to be ready. They were anxious to climb from that railroad coach and know that the long ride was ended.

Joey and I sat quietly. Even my complacent young brother was a little scared now; I could see it in the sudden paleness of his face. Lonnie's kitchen seemed very far away; the happiness and security we'd felt there was very precious. We were coming home, our own and not a borrowed home. We should have been eager and excited, but we weren't. We were scared.

Our train entered the great smoke-stained station at last, slowly, majestically, as incoming trains so often seemed to move. The sunlight could reach the inside of the station only in narrow panels of light here and there, light that contrasted with the gloom of the long vista which we were entering.

"Chicago!" the conductor shouted to us as the train came to a stop. He warned us not to forget our parcels.

Joey looked up at me. "I guess they'll meet us, won't they?" he asked in a small voice.

"I think they will," I answered. I felt sick.

Slowly we made our way out of the coach. Down the length of the train people were pouring from a dozen coaches, limping under the weight of their baggage toward the station at the end of the platform. People were standing at the doors of the station watching for those they had come to meet. Almost immediately I saw Mom standing there with Kitty at her side. A second later I saw Dad, only a few feet from us, scanning the crowd that was getting off the coach, just ahead of ours.

The old impulse to criticize him, to be angry with him, flashed through my mind. "Sure, Mom and Kitty must wait in the background; the lord and master must be first." Then, shamed as I looked at him, I thought, "For Heaven's sake, give the poor guy a chance; you're not perfect yourself, you know."

He hadn't spotted us, and we had a chance to see what the winter had done to him as we walked slowly toward him. He had been so big, so strong, and he was now thin and stooped with great hollows in his cheeks. There in his face were the lines of his suffering. I couldn't have been callous enough at that moment to feel angry or critical of him as he stood there, his face pleading that Joey and I would be the next to appear at the door of that coach.

We walked up to him, and I touched his arm. "Hello, Dad. Sure is good to see you again," I said.

He gave a start of surprise, and then his face

lighted up in recognition. With his left arm he drew Joey to him; with his right hand he clasped my hand firmly.

"Hello, Son," he said. "I'm so glad—so glad—" He ducked his head a little, turning his face away from me as I had turned away from Joey the night Lonnie brought him home. Tears were not in Dad's pattern either.

Góralu! Czy Ci Nie Żal?

Góralu! czy ci nie żal ? Góralu!   wróć   się   do   hal !
Highlander! do you not regret? Highlander! come back to the meadows!